D0291981

CHILDREN OF THE STONE CITY

Burn My Heart

Journey to Jo'burg

No Turning Back

Out of Bounds

The Other Side of Truth

Web of Lies

Beverley Naidoo

CHILDREN OF THE STONE CITY

Quill Tree Books
An Imprint of HarperCollinsPublishers

Quill Tree Books is an imprint of HarperCollins Publishers.

Children of the Stone City

www.harpercollinschildrens.com

Library of Congress Cataloging-in-Publication Data
Names: Naidoo, Beverley, author.
Title: Children of the Stone City / Beverley Naidoo.
Description: First edition. | New York : Quill Tree Books, [2022] | Audience: Ages 10 up. | Audience: Grades 7-9. | Summary: "In a city where people are divided into Permitteds and Nons, music-loving Adam and his younger sister Leila must navigate the dangers of being second-class citizens and decide how to stand up for their rights."—Provided by publisher.
Identifiers: LCCN 2021057382 | ISBN 978-0-06-309696-7 (hardcover)
Subjects: LCSH: Discrimination—Juvenile fiction. | Brothers and sisters—Juvenile fiction. | Child musicians—Juvenile fiction. | Mothers—Juvenile fiction. | CYAC: Discrimination—Fiction. | Brothers and sisters—Fiction. | Musicians—Fiction. | Mothers—Fiction. | LCGFT: Fiction. | Novels.
Classification: LCC PZ7.N1384 Cj 2022 | DDC 823.914 [Fic]--dc23/eng/20220510
LC record available at https://lccn.loc.gov/2021057382

Typography by Molly Fehr
22 23 24 25 26 PC/LSCH 10 9 8 7 6 5 4 3 2 1

First Edition

To all my grandchildren and the young
dream-makers of a shared world without Permitteds
and Nons—and where weapons of war are
transformed into musical instruments.

Hope is being able to see that there is light
despite all of the darkness.
—Desmond Tutu

The bow flies over the strings and his violin sings. . . .

He's flying bareback over ancient hills, like Grandfather Tomas in the Time Before . . . a boy on a chestnut stallion with a mane glowing in the sun. A bird dives into the valley below . . . a flash of emerald calling, "Follow! Follow!" The boy guides his horse down terraces of olive trees. The horse's nostrils quiver. There's water ahead, in a meadow of wild-flowers. "Go, my friend!" he whispers . . . and they canter to the spring.

ADAM

"WATCH IT!"

ADAM ZIGZAGGED THROUGH THE CROWD, his violin case clutched against his chest. The soundtrack in his head was so dazzling, he could only dream of being good enough to play the solo himself. Ever since he'd heard the melody at last year's concert, he had loved it.

"Not so fast!" gasped Leila. She struggled to stay close to her brother as they entered the Great Gate, but he didn't hear. Even when they emerged in the noisy marketplace inside the Stone City, he was in such a hurry to turn onto the cobbled side street that he didn't see the Permitted policeman on horseback until too late.

"Adam!" Leila grabbed the blue canvas schoolbag on his shoulder. His violin case swung around, narrowly missing the horse's front shin, and collided into her flute case. For a moment, Adam saw his own fright mirrored in the shining eye of the horse. The policeman's eyes were hidden behind dark glasses.

"Watch it!" barked the Permitted, tugging sharply on the reins. He steered the huge stallion around the children. Its body was midnight black except for two white shins and a white arrow down its forehead. For a moment, Adam felt sympathy for the harnessed creature, until he remembered seeing a woman's foot crushed by a horse like this one.

A second mounted policeman now appeared from the side street. With their backs against a stone wall, the children watched people move aside. Most were Nons like themselves. There were also tourists with their cameras, bags, and hats, some smiling at the police on horseback as if watching a quaint custom.

"You won't say anything, will you?" Adam's voice hovered between plea and demand. He fixed his eyes ahead, not wanting his sister to see he was still shaken. Almost thirteen, he was two years older than Leila. How many times had he been told not to be such a dreamer? *You need to be more practical like your sister.* What could he say if asked why he hadn't looked before dashing into a Permitted police horse? How could he say that he'd been playing Vivaldi's "Spring" in his head? Or that he'd been imagining himself, like his grandfather in the Time Before, riding freely through valleys and over hills on a chestnut horse?

"Of course not!" Leila combed her fingers through her jet-black bangs and deliberately widened her eyes, as if to say, *Who do you think I am?*

They both knew that there was more than enough to worry about at home. It was always in the weeks leading up to Easter that Dad began preparing to apply for Mama's annual permit to remain with them. Without her permit, Mama would be sent back to the other side of the Concrete Wall . . . back to the town where she was born. She might never be allowed back again. This certainly wasn't the time for other complications, like their son being accused of injuring a Permitted police horse!

Adam slowed down to Leila's pace. It was only ten minutes to walk home through the narrow back alleys rather than the main thoroughfare. Either way involved climbing up uneven steps of stone, furrowed from centuries of use. The limestone walls on each side changed color from soft browns and grays to pink, yellow, and even white in bright sunlight. Sometimes Adam would think of a piece of music that invisibly shifted in mood from dark to light or light to dark. But today, after nearly crashing into the police horse, he just listened to Leila go on about her flute class and answered her questions about the junior orchestra.

They avoided using the alleys where Permitted flags hung out of windows in houses that not long ago had belonged to Non families.

At least there weren't any flags yet in the alley with the little yellow parakeet. Now that it was spring, the parakeet's owner hung the cage in an open window, and Leila insisted on stopping for a "chat" through the bars. The parakeet's squeaky "allo-allo" made them both laugh. They were still mimicking it when they reached the steps below the stone doorway of Grandma's house. Home.

They were greeted by the smell of freshly baked cookies, still in the pan on the counter that separated the small kitchen from their living room. Grandma rightly described the design as "cozy."

"Welcome," Mama greeted them. "Perfect timing!" Steam rose from two cups of mint tea on the table in front of her and Grandma in the living room. It was Mama's day off from her voluntary work at the library, and they had been baking.

"Come. Sit." Grandma began to push herself up, but Mama gently restrained her.

"I'll see to the children," she said, before turning to them. "Only two cookies each now. It'll soon be dinner. Your father's coming home early."

They didn't need to ask why. The reminder was right in front of them. Mama's bright red shoebox sat perched at the end of the kitchen counter, near the pan of cookies. Dad had left it there this morning, brimming with papers.

A gas bill and a water bill were still missing to complete the papers he needed to present at the Permitted Department of the Interior. The department officials insisted on seeing *every* item, *every* year. They wanted to see new documents and also old ones that Dad had shown many times before, like Mama's birth certificate, their marriage certificate, and the lease agreement for Grandma's house in the Stone City, which was now in Dad's name. He was the oldest of Grandma's children and the only one still living in the Stone City.

The red shoebox had once housed Mama's wedding shoes. Using it for his "filing system" showed how ridiculous Dad found these Permitted checks on Mama's right to be with her family. But on the day of the interview he would transfer all the papers into his tan leather briefcase. It wasn't worth testing an official's sense of humor.

THE EMPTY CHAIR

WHEN ADAM'S FATHER HADN'T COME home by dinnertime, Mama rang his cell phone. Dad didn't answer, so she left a message. *Where are you?* Then she phoned his office. No answer. Everyone must have left.

"This isn't like your father, not to let us know," said Mama. The phone slipped from her fingers, clattering onto the table. Adam glimpsed a frown pass over Grandma's forehead. She was carefully setting down a large dish of rice next to the carrot salad. "Sit down, Mother, while I get the rest," Mama continued, "and wash your hands, children. We'd better start."

Dad's chair stayed empty throughout dinner. Grandma ate in silence, but Mama kept asking Adam and Leila one question after another. She even repeated questions she had asked earlier. What had they done at school? What did they do at music school? Were there any problems on the way home? How was it at the Gate? Were there more police than usual? It was as if Mama was hoping their answers might fill the empty chair.

But after they finished eating, Mama snapped.

"You'd better practice your flute, young lady." Her voice was unusually sharp. Leila's eyes welled up. Adam saw a red spot bobbing across each of Mama's cheeks.

Grandma broke her silence. "It will be all right. He is a careful man."

"It's not whether *he* is careful, Mother! We all know that."

Drawing in a long slow breath, Grandma pushed herself up from her seat.

"Come." She stretched out a hand to Leila. "I'd like to listen to your new piece." Adam's sister managed half a smile.

Grandma's pink slippers shuffled as they made their way across the faded carpet and limestone floor to the bedroom she shared with Leila. Adam felt the silence bearing down on him as the door shut. How could Mama be so abrupt, especially to their grandmother? It wasn't like her. Whenever Adam's temper started rising, it was Mama who reminded him of their father's saying: *Use your head as well as your heart to stop an explosion.* She must be really worried. For the first time that evening, Adam felt scared.

He was tempted to retreat to his bedroom. He could

escape with his violin. But then he'd feel guilty about leaving his mother to worry alone. After rummaging through his backpack, he spread out his geography textbook and an exercise book on the table. If Dad were home, he would help. As an archaeologist, he knew a lot about how humans lived in the past as well as about how to date layers of earth when excavating. He was always ready to discuss questions of history and geography with Adam. Sometimes Mama, Grandma, or even Leila joined in. Everything felt different tonight and Mama said nothing as she washed the dishes. However, the way she glanced every now and again at Adam told him that she was glad he was there.

Fifteen minutes later, Mama perched on the edge of the settee as she called one of Dad's colleagues. Adam pretended to read while trying to fill in the gaps of the conversation.

"Did he mention a late meeting? . . . I know you don't travel this way, but have you heard of any trouble? . . . Yes, our neighbors are very good. Whenever we're out, they check on his mother." The dip in his mother's voice made him take a sideways peek. When he saw her lift her eyes to the ceiling, Adam knew she wasn't getting any useful information. ". . . No, nothing different from the usual hassles . . . Please let me know if you get any news . . . Yes, thank you."

Mama sighed and called someone else. The conversation was similar but not in Non. Mama spoke Permitted, although not as fluently as Dad, who used both languages for work. She must be speaking to a Permitted colleague in his father's department, which made Adam look directly at her. After replacing the receiver, his mother's shoulders slumped, and her arms hung down at her sides. For a moment he thought of broken wings.

"No one knows where your father is. They say he left after a meeting. Stay by the phone, Adam, while I check with our neighbors."

"They'd have come here, Mama, if they'd heard anything. Zak would have told us if there was trouble!"

It was a family joke that their neighbor's son, Zak, with his skateboard and his ear for gossip, was the world's fastest postman. But Mama was already halfway out the door and didn't turn back. If anyone could find out what had happened, it would be Zak's father, Uncle Musa. His family had lived in the same house for generations and he knew everyone. Uncle Musa was also their closest family in the Stone City even though they weren't related. Adam had heard him and Dad each declare that different religions would never stop them from being brothers, whatever any Permitted might say.

Adam recognized the tune of Beethoven's "Ode to Joy" coming from Leila's flute in Grandma's bedroom. It was one of Mama's favorites, which she sang with her choir. She must be pleased that Leila was learning it. Adam tried to concentrate on his work, but his mind kept wandering to the empty chair opposite him and to the photograph on the wall behind it. It showed their father on his nineteenth birthday. He stood tall, between his parents, in front of a stone doorway. Dad gazed seriously at the camera, with a strained smile beneath his narrow mustache. Only a few hours before the picture was taken, he had been released from a Permitted prison, where he had been held for two years with other Nons. Whenever Adam looked at this photograph, he could hear his father's voice. *Of course I was happy to come home. But I couldn't stop thinking of the friends I had left behind.*

Five minutes later, the telephone rang. At last! Dad! The flute music stopped as Adam lifted the receiver. It was a lady asking to speak with their mother. Adam dashed out of the house to collect Mama.

The rest of the night was long and painful. From the moment of the phone call, Adam's heart began beating like the rolling of timpani drums. Mama hurried back with Zak's father. Grandma bowed her head as Mama repeated words. *Hospital? Heart attack? On the bus?* When Mama asked how her husband was now, she was just told to come straight away. Zak's father arranged for his brother to collect them with his taxi. Grandma insisted on hobbling with them despite her bad knee. Adam and Leila squeezed themselves between Grandma and Mama on the back seat. Uncle Musa sat in the passenger seat. He kept repeating that Dad was like another brother to him and he couldn't believe what had happened. The timpani drums continued beating inside Adam.

Once they were out of the Stone City, the journey to the Non hospital seemed to take forever through the night traffic. To make matters worse, it began raining and the heavens opened as they scrambled into the hospital's entrance hall. A nun in a charcoal-gray tunic and veil was waiting for them. Sister Joseph introduced herself, greeting them each quietly.

"I'm so sorry." Her voice was little more than a whisper. "The driver drove his bus right to our door. We did our best, but God made his decision. We couldn't save him."

We couldn't save him. The words echoed as they followed Sister Joseph down a long, brightly lit corridor before she shepherded them into a side room. Adam clustered with his family as they stepped nearer the bed. He felt Grandma lean on him while Leila clasped Mama's hand. Could Dad not just be sleeping under the blanket? But when Sister Joseph carefully removed the cover, it looked like a mask of gray wax had been poured over their father's face. There was no escape from the terrible truth.

In her office, they learned as much as Sister Joseph herself knew. Dad had collapsed while standing on a crowded bus on his way home. When passengers alerted the driver, he diverted from his usual route to the hospital. As the adults continued talking, they too seemed to disappear behind masks. Adam's mind shut down.

UNCLE ELIAS

UNCLE ELIAS WAS DAD'S ONLY sibling allowed to come to the funeral. All Grandma's children, except for Dad, had left to live more freely in other countries. Uncle Elias lived the farthest away, in the country that had once been the OverPower governing everyone. He was Grandma's youngest child and was a writer. He had never married, and Grandma seemed to worry about him the most.

Dad's two married sisters were both desperate to come home for the funeral. They lived much nearer than Uncle Elias, just across the Permitteds' Outer Border. But when Mama and Grandma spoke with them online, they were tearful. The Permitteds had said no. Mama said that it was only Uncle Elias's passport from the old OverPower that got him in. Although Grandma's children had all been born in this old stone house in the Stone City, the Permitteds wouldn't allow them even to visit for a few days.

"Inhuman!" Zak's mother breathed sharply on hearing this news. Aunt Nadia and Zak had brought two pots with an evening meal for Adam's family. Her indigo headscarf quivered as she shook her head. However, Grandma changed the conversation by asking about Aunt Nadia's mother. Zak's grandmother was her oldest friend . . . and this was Grandma's way of coping.

No one from Mama's family was allowed to come to the funeral. They lived nearest of all, in the town where Mama had been born. The Permitteds still had control over their lives, and now that they had built the Concrete Wall between Mama's hometown and the city, any Non from the other side of the Wall needed special permission to enter the city. It hadn't always been that way. When Mama was a child, her family had often visited the Stone City. The old stones held their Non history and it was where they used to meet up with family members from elsewhere to celebrate special occasions. Mama and her young cousins had especially loved the Easter Sunday parade. But the Permitteds stopped that with their Wall, making life as difficult as possible for Nons on both sides, and Mama knew there was no point in anyone from her family trying to get a permit in time to attend the funeral. Instead, she spent hours late at night on the computer, talking and writing to them.

Her red shoebox was a constant reminder that she herself required permission each year to remain in the Stone City, even with her own children.

Other neighbors and friends rallied around as well. At times, everything felt unreal to Adam, as if they were in a play. In the first week after Dad's death, the old stone house filled with people coming to say how sad and shocked they were. Like Zak's family, some brought dishes of food, and others offered whatever help they could. A small group from Dad's archaeology department came to pay their respects, including a Permitted colleague who told Grandma how much he had admired Dad's work. Adam heard him say, "It was a privilege to work with such a fine archaeologist." He spoke slowly in Non and Adam watched Grandma raise her eyes, nodding silently before quietly saying, "Thank you." Adam's own eyes blurred, fighting back tears.

In the second week, after the funeral, the house filled with friends of Uncle Elias. They usually stayed longer, wanting to talk with him. Uncle Musa also remained late one night, telling the long story of how Dad had helped him go to court each time that a group of Permitteds had tried to evict his widowed sister, Hala, and her family from their house in the alley around the corner. Adam knew how the Permitteds claimed that the house had once belonged to a Permitted family and said it was their right to take it back. Although Dad had helped Uncle Musa find documents to show that Nons had been living there for at least a hundred years, the claimants still hadn't given up. When Adam couldn't keep his eyes open any longer, he went to bed with Uncle Musa's words in his head: "That's why I always say your father was my brother."

Another night, Mama stayed up very late talking with Uncle Elias. Grandma and Leila left for their bedroom and, more than once, Mama told Adam to go as well. But Uncle Elias intervened, saying that Adam was now "the man of the house." He would have to grow up fast. It was best that he know everything, including Mama's concerns. How would she renew her permit to stay without Dad? How would they live without Dad's income? As a Non born on the other side of the Concrete Wall, Mama wasn't permitted to work. She could only do voluntary work. Uncle Elias tried to reassure Mama.

"Musa and I will find a lawyer to help with the permit, and I'll send money to keep you all going in the meantime," he promised. He turned to Adam. "You and Leila must both continue with your music lessons. Your father would have wanted that."

Adam wanted to say something, but the words became tangled in his throat. Dad often said he regretted not learning to play the violin when he was younger. *Your grandfather could have taught me, but with all the problems we faced, I thought it was a luxury. I was wrong.*

Later, as Adam lay on his mattress, questions tossed in his mind. If Mama were sent away, what would happen to him and Leila? They were born on this side of the Permitteds' Concrete Wall, but how could they live without Mama? They couldn't! Moreover, once they were on the other side of the Wall, the Permitteds might never let them back to where they'd been born and everything they loved, including music school! Grandma was also too old to look after them . . . and she would never leave her house to come with them. She had been uprooted once before with her family when she was a young girl, and the horror of that memory had never left her. Leaving Grandma alone in her stone house was unthinkable. Then there were questions of money. How long could Uncle Elias keep them "all going" with his money? Grandma already worried about him and didn't think being a writer was "steady enough." So how could he manage their school fees *and* music lessons on top of everything?

Adam's brain felt ready to burst with so many unanswered problems. Why, oh why, did Dad have to die? Why a heart attack? Dad wasn't even old! He had always tried to keep fit. He loved walking. When they couldn't go out into the hills, he would often take Adam and Leila early on a Sunday morning through the maze of streets in the Stone City. He would tell them about different places. He told stories about adventures with friends when growing up . . . and much older stories from long ago. *Our stories help make our history. Don't let's forget them. Do you understand, children?* How often had Dad said that?

Adam's eyelids were wet. He didn't want to be the man of the house! He just wanted Dad back! Drawing up his knees, Adam clutched his arms around his stomach. If only he could take out his violin and play for a while, it would calm him . . . but that would wake everyone up. It was finally in the early hours of the morning, when his mind was exhausted, that Adam fell asleep.

The next morning, Uncle Elias said Mama's permit was now their "priority." Mama emptied the contents of the red shoebox into Dad's briefcase, and Uncle Musa escorted them to see the Non lawyer who was trying to stop his sister from being evicted. On their return, Mama explained that the lawyer had made copies of all the papers and said he would submit her application. If Mama was called for an interview, he would accompany her. The lawyer couldn't say how long it would take or how the Permitted authorities would respond. But he would do his best.

As the time drew nearer for Uncle Elias to leave, Grandma's eyes would suddenly well up like springs of clear blue water, while Leila's eyes reminded Adam of freshly washed dates. By now, Mama's face gave the impression of a desert. It was as if she had cried away all her tears.

On Uncle Elias's last night, Mama made her special upside-down dish of rice, eggplant, and chicken. It had always been Dad's favorite. She held a plate tightly on top of the pot before turning it over and setting it down carefully in the middle of the table. Dad was usually the first to place one hand lightly on the upturned pot, followed by everyone else. Their hands would fan out like petals and they would let the food settle for a couple of minutes, joking about how perfect Mama's "cake" would turn out. Tonight, there was a moment's silence before their mother raised her hand and placed it on the pot.

"Come," she invited the family. "Let's keep our tradition." One by one, Uncle Elias, the children, and Grandma each added a hand. They remained quiet. Everyone was surely remembering Dad.

Later, Adam sat in bed, propped against his pillow. From his bookshelf, he had pulled out the last book that Dad had bought for him. It was a collection of folktales. Dad had explained that the stories came from a country that once had a huge empire, just like the OverPower, so the stories may have traveled over vast distances. Adam turned to the title page, where his father had written a message. . . .

We're never too old for these stories, son. Like bits of pottery we find in the earth, they tell us something about the people who made them. Maybe the people inside the stories are not all that different from us today, with the same nightmares, dreams, and hopes.

Love, Dad

Adam especially liked "The Firebird and the Horse of Power." It was similar to one of Grandma's old Non tales where the unfavored son of a king is given a number of impossible tasks but a jinn horse saves him. Adam had just reached the horse of power's warning to the young man not to pick up the firebird's feather when there was a soft knock at the door.

"It's just me," Uncle Elias said as he came in quietly. The book closed swiftly between Adam's hands. "What are you reading?" Adam hesitated a second before turning over the book's cover with the jinn horse stamping on the firebird's tail.

"Ah! Your father always loved stories like this. When I was little, he would tell me about flying horses that would take you anywhere you wished! For a while, I even believed him!"

Adam wanted to hear more, but instead Uncle Elias now pulled out two leather-bound books from a paper bag. He placed them on the bed. Each was embossed with a different pattern.

"These are for you and Leila. The pages are blank," he said, handing one to Adam. "Whatever you write in here, it's for you, yourself. Treat this book like a special friend and just be honest when you write." He sounded so much like Dad that Adam felt hot tears pricking.

"When your dad was twelve, like you, and I was ten, like Leila, our favorite uncle gave each of us a diary for Christmas."

"What did Dad write in his?"

"Your father was passionate about making lists! He made a new one every day."

"About what?"

"Almost anything! The singers he liked, their songs, famous soccer players, or even what he had to remember for a test in school."

Adam smiled. That fit. Dad was always jotting down things in a notebook that he kept in the top pocket of his gray jacket.

"And when there was trouble, he counted the soldiers and police on the way to school and listed them in a code that only the two of us knew. He turned them into lists."

Adam wanted to hear more about his father when he was young, but Uncle Elias had begun talking about how he had used his own book.

"I used it like a trusted friend. You can do the same. Just write what's happening, Adam! Write what you're feeling, thinking. Tell it like it is. Later on, this habit stopped me from going mad when the Permitteds . . ." Uncle Elias's voice trailed off and he looked away. He had done that quite a lot in the past two weeks. But when his uncle looked away, Adam's voice also dried up. As Uncle Elias wished him good night, he put his broad hands on Adam's shoulders. That, too, was so like Dad.

"I know how you love your music, Adam," he said softly. "Your grandfather would be very pleased. You know that he also recited poetry? Your words can make music too."

The lump in Adam's throat burst as soon as he heard the door click. Alone, under his duvet, he swallowed his sobs.

GONE

How do I begin?
"Tell it like it is."

Uncle Elias leaves before dawn,
worried about missing his plane.
Anything can happen at a checkpoint.

Grandma whispers,
"When shall we see you again?"
Her fingers stroke his cheeks
like feathers.
"I'll try, Mother, I'll try
to come back before long."
His eyes linger
on each of us.
"Take good care of yourselves,"
he says gently.

Zak's father insists
he must carry
Uncle's suitcase to the car.
We say our goodbyes
with hugs and kisses
and watch them disappear
into the shadows of our alley.

Grandma bows her head
as church bells strike the air.
Like any other morning
they follow the first call to prayer.

But this is not like any other morning.

ZAK

ZAK APPEARED AT THE DOOR as they were finishing breakfast. He carried his skateboard under one arm. This was the first time he had brought it with him since Dad's death. It had been made by one of Uncle Musa's carpenter friends. That was less than a year ago and already Zak was doing tricks like a professional.

"Come. Eat something." Grandma pointed to a chair. Adam knew how she worried that Zak, only a few months older than Adam, was so skinny and that his family couldn't afford to eat as healthily as they did.

Zak put up his hand with a polite no but came to sit at the table next to Adam. "Thank you, Grandma. I'm fine."

Grandma constantly worried about others. She was like a grandmother to Zak too. She and Zak's grandmother were friends from long ago. As girls, they had lived at opposite ends of the same village and first met at the village well, each of them drawing water to carry home. Sometimes they forgot the time and got into trouble. Their different religions never got in the way of their friendship. However, when Permitted fighters had come over the hills with guns to take their village, the two families had fled to different places and the girls lost touch with each other. Many years later, when Zak's grandmother came to live with her married daughter in the Stone City, the two old ladies had been overjoyed to find themselves neighbors.

"How is your grandmother?" Grandma always asked this even though the two friends spoke to each other almost every day.

"She says she didn't sleep last night because she was thinking of you saying goodbye to Uncle." Grandma lowered her eyes. Adam suspected they were welling up again.

Zak now turned to Mama, who was making more coffee. His fingers fiddled with the skateboard on his lap. "The shop isn't open today, Aunty. Can Adam come to the park with me?"

Zak spent Saturdays and occasional days after school running errands for a mini-market near the Great Gate. It was owned by a friend of Uncle Musa's, and Zak was proud of the little bit of extra money he brought home every week.

Mama hesitated. Her gaze shifted toward Dad's old chair. In the past, she would have checked what he thought. "Why is the shop shut?" Mama asked.

"Maybe some problem with the permit. . . ." Zak flipped over one hand in a gesture of *Who knows?* Removal of a permit, without any warning, could happen anytime.

"So which park will you go to?" Mama wasn't letting up. She must know, thought Adam, but she was giving herself time to decide.

There was only one small nearby park that Nons could use. It was outside the Stone City's walls, not far from Zak's school and also near their music school. After their music lessons, Zak often came skimming on his skateboard toward Adam and Leila down the narrow street, veering between cars and pedestrians. He would flip up his board outside the iron gates and, with a grin, suggest they walk home through the park. It wasn't much farther that way and gave him a chance to display any clever new footwork. In the park, Zak always offered each of them a turn. Adam didn't like to admit it, but his sister was more confident than he was. He never told Zak about his fear that, if he fell off, he might break an arm. Even breaking a finger would be awful. Then how could he play his violin? Zak would probably say he could teach him how to fall. But Adam held back and was always happy to let Leila take longer on the skateboard.

"Can I go with them, Mama?" Leila chimed in suddenly. She had lost all her usual bounce since Dad died and had hardly even spoken since Uncle Elias left. Adam was jolted by Mama's swift response.

"No. We've had many visitors and there's a lot of cleaning up to do."

"But—" Leila began.

"No buts. I need you here, young lady." Mama's voice sharpened and Adam knew there was no chance of persuading her otherwise. Mama turned to Adam and Zak.

"I expect you boys to be back by one o'clock. Adam, you have to prepare for school and practice your music this afternoon. You've a lot to catch up on. Make sure you're not late . . . and be careful! Remember, you have only one set of hands."

"I won't be late, Mama!" Adam felt himself blush. He needed to get away before Mama embarrassed him openly in front of Zak by saying that he shouldn't go on the skateboard without proper gloves. She had gone on about this not long ago, asking, "How will you play your violin if you damage your hands?" Dad had calmed her by promising to get Adam some protective gloves and elbow pads. Adam also knew he'd feel safer with them. Now, of course, they'd be too expensive.

As he slipped away from the table, Adam saw his sister's face crumple. Mama had sounded so harsh. Surely Dad would have trusted Leila with him and Zak? Or, if Dad wasn't busy, he might have come with all three of them, enjoying the chance to relax. But Adam quashed those thoughts. It was hard enough coping with his own misery. At least for a couple of hours, he was free to get out of the house, where the pang of missing Dad lurked in every room. He would try to practice his balance on Zak's skateboard. One thing he knew for sure: he would never rival his friend's skill. When it came to skateboarding, Zak was king.

THE PARK

"WHICH WAY?" ZAK STOOD IN the road below the house, swinging his forefinger like the pendulum of a metronome. Adam hesitated. The Great Gate would be the shortest route, but he hadn't forgotten his collision with the police horse. The busier the gate, the more chance of police. He flicked his thumb in the direction of the Northwest Gate. "Not so many people this way."

Almost as soon as Adam's words were out, Zak whizzed past, swishing one hand just past Adam's nose. Farther down the street, Zak stopped and swung around.

"Tell me when you want a turn!" he shouted.

Adam raised his right thumb. Zak knew that he wouldn't take up the offer until they were in the park, but he always liked to be fair. Zak set off again and Adam followed at a jog. Sometimes Zak disappeared behind people far ahead, but he would always skate back to wave to Adam before disappearing again.

When Adam turned the corner toward the Northwest Gate, however, he couldn't see his friend. He stopped jogging beside a row of shops to catch his breath. After a short while, he wondered whether Zak had already gone through the gate. A pair of Permitted police stood chatting to each other near the gateway. Adam began walking toward it when, suddenly, Zak leaped out from behind the wooden shutter of one of the shops. He swiveled the skateboard in midair, landing with a great clank to face Adam.

"Duh-daah!" Zak twirled his arms and hands like a circus acrobat.

His trick startled the other pedestrians too. They were all Nons, and although a group of young men began to laugh, an older couple looked disapproving.

"You can hurt people on that crazy thing!" the man warned angrily.

"You'll hurt yourself too if you aren't more careful!" added the woman, probably his wife.

Zak lowered his head with his dark curly hair swaying over his eyes.

"Sorry, sorry!" he mumbled. Quickly, he picked up his skateboard and wedged it under his arm.

"Let's go," he said to Adam, nodding toward the gate. The policemen were still busy chatting. That was lucky, thought Adam. It didn't take much for them to stir up a storm in a coffee cup, as Grandma might say. But Zak was more concerned about the unsmiling Non couple.

"If they find out who my father is, that's it!" Zak whispered urgently. He sliced the air with his spare hand. "He'll take my skateboard away!"

"I'll explain that you were just playing a trick on me . . . and it wasn't *so* bad," Adam assured him.

"He'll believe the adults more!"

Adam said nothing. It was true. Moreover, Uncle Musa quite often told Zak off for being impetuous. It was especially embarrassing when Adam was present because Uncle Musa would add, "Why can't you be more sensible like Adam here?" Another time, Adam overheard Zak's mother tell Mama that she lay awake at night worrying about Zak. Aunt Nadia wished Adam could influence him to become calmer. Adam had wanted to call out that he couldn't change his friend's personality! Besides, Zak created the kind of madcap fun that he didn't have with anyone else. Most of his antics were just a bit silly, not really dangerous. But it was also true that, living where they did, even something quite innocent could suddenly turn dangerous.

As soon as they were on the other side of the Northwest Gate, Zak released a sound like steam from Grandma's pressure cooker.

"That man spoke to me like he was a Permitted! I didn't touch them, or anyone else!"

"No, you didn't," Adam murmured. It was best to let Zak cool down. An empty sidewalk stretched downhill. Zak tossed down his skateboard.

"I'll see you at the park," he called, speeding off. Adam watched him curve to left and right in long flowing swoops. A thought crossed his mind. Maybe Zak escaped on his skateboard like Adam did sometimes with his violin, like being somewhere else and quite free, just for a while. Adam set off at his own pace in a slow jog down the hill.

The two boys had played together since they were babies, or so Mama said. When she had arrived as a new bride to live in Grandma's house, Zak's mother had taken her under her wing, introducing her to family and friends, as well as to the best stallholders in the market. Mama had added, "We really liked each other. This was a blessing because marrying your father meant that I had to leave all my family and friends behind the Wall."

Zak had been born first, and Adam seven months later. The two families remained close and, as they grew, the children played in each other's homes while their mothers and grandmas chatted, cooked, and baked. Their different festivals were special times for enjoying each family's best dishes. While Adam's sister, Leila, was born a couple of years after him, Zak remained an only child. As Adam grew, he understood that this was linked to a sadness that the adults didn't speak about openly. Zak was loved by his family and looked up to by younger cousins.

At six years old, the two boys had been sent to different schools. Adam joined the school his father had attended as a scholarship student. His father's good job meant he could pay the full fees for Adam. When Adam had asked why Zak couldn't attend the same school, Dad had explained that Zak's family couldn't afford it. Typical of Dad, he hadn't stopped there. *It's not Uncle Musa's fault that he doesn't earn enough. He's a fine carpenter and works very hard. You must never judge anyone by how much money they have.*

The time that the boys spent in each other's homes, or in the nearby courtyard playing soccer, gradually became less frequent. Adam's teachers gave more homework, and by the time he was eight there were music lessons as well. Although their families remained close, they might have grown apart. Yet both boys still enjoyed spending time together. This included keeping up their friendly rivalry at checkers where their sharpness was equally matched. Adam could relax with Zak and, while his friend had always been more boisterous, Adam continued to admire Zak's nerve, even when he was being a bit of a showman.

Zak was standing at the park entrance, flipping the tail of his skateboard with his right foot. Each time the deck stood upright, he caught the nose end with his right hand, displaying his collection of stickers. It had taken him a year to collect enough boldly colored dinosaurs, dragons, and skeletons on skateboards to cover the underside.

"Slowpoke!" Zak chuckled as Adam arrived, panting up the hill.

"I'll bring my Ferrari next time!" jibed Adam, not rising to the bait. He was happy that Zak's mood had lifted.

"Here!" Zak held out his skateboard. "Shall I teach you to ollie today?"

Adam took the skateboard and together they walked up the steps into the park. "Thanks, but not yet! Let me get the basics right first."

With his music, Adam had always been taught to start with "the basics." This meant how to stand, how to hold his violin, and how to grip his bow. Even before his scales, he had to play on each open string to make sure it was in tune. Although Adam had tried Zak's skateboard before, he still needed to feel surer of his balance and learn how to gather speed without falling off. Tricks would have to come later.

Zak arched his eyebrows. "Not scared, are you?"

Adam stared in silence at the tarmac path ahead of them, winding its way across the park. Was Zak laughing at him? He wanted to tell Zak, "You don't understand what hurting an arm, wrist, or finger would mean for me!" But it might sound like he was showing off. Zak didn't play a musical instrument. His parents couldn't afford violin lessons.

"Come on, Adam! I heard what your mother said. She's like mine. They worry too much!" Zak wasn't giving up. Then he added, "Leila was learning how to ollie last time we came here. She's really good!"

Adam bristled. Dad had been with them that last time . . . sitting next to him on the bench as they'd watched Zak give Leila a lesson. After her final jump off the skateboard, Leila had flashed smiles all around, while Dad had laughed and clapped. Adam pushed the memory aside.

"So? We're different! You don't need to compare us." He placed the skateboard down on the path. The wheels clattered against the tarmac surface.

"Sorry! Sorry!" Zak raised his hands. "The ollie is the most *basic* trick, so I thought you'd like to learn it!" He paused and shrugged. "Tell me when you're ready, then!" With that, he sauntered off in the direction of a group of boys playing soccer.

Adam stood frowning at the skateboard in front of him. He'd thought it would be good to get away from the house with all the sorrow, but first there had been the couple who were cross with Zak, and now Zak seemed to be cross with *him*! Yet Zak couldn't be too upset, because he'd still left him with his prize possession.

Relax! It's okay! Out of the blue, Dad's voice felt close. Adam glanced around. For an instant, his vision blurred. If Dad were watching him now from the nearby bench, he'd be leaning back with folded arms and a gentle smile, putting Adam at ease. Yet Dad's steady brown eyes, under his thick graying eyebrows, were also sentinels and prepared for anything. Adam pushed back his tears, letting himself respond to Dad's advice. *Relax! It's okay!*

With a deep breath, Adam placed his right foot on the deck of the skateboard, slightly bending his knee to be closer to the ground. Then he pushed off lightly with his left foot. As the skateboard rolled forward, his arms rose sideways to help his balance. The ground was quite even so he could control his speed with his left foot. Luckily, the path ahead was empty. The rough noise of the wheels seemed to create a sound bubble around him that helped his focus.

When Adam reached the other end of the park, he stopped with his left foot and turned around. If he could just practice like this on his own for a while, he would become more confident. Sure enough, his left foot soon began pushing a little harder. He continued traveling across the park, back and forth, until, suddenly, he felt ready to put his left foot up on the deck behind his right. Amazing! The skateboard rolled on with both his feet off the ground!

"Hey, Adam!" Zak's voice made him glance in the direction of the soccer players. Zak had raised his thumbs up in the air. It looked like he was making his peace. Adam smiled and lifted both thumbs on his outstretched hands. *Thanks, Dad*, he replied silently to the voice in his head.

GRANDFATHER'S VIOLIN

THE FIRST THING THAT ADAM saw when he returned through the stone doorway was Grandfather Tomas's violin case, open on the settee, flanked by Grandma's hand-embroidered cushions. The violin's scroll was carved as a splendid horsehead that peered above the neatly sewn purple blanket protecting the strings. Normally the old violin lay tucked inside its case on top of the cupboard in Grandma's bedroom. She brought it down once a year as part of her Easter spring cleaning. But Easter was still a couple of weeks away.

No one else was in the room as Adam sat down and lifted the soft purple covering. Grandfather used to play his violin every day. Even at the end of his life, propped against pillows in bed, he liked to tuck it under his chin.

His left hand could barely hold up the instrument and his right hand trembled as he raised the bow. He would try to tune the strings and play a few notes of an old Non tune. Adam was just six at the time, but he still carried a picture in his head of Grandfather in bed with his violin, his eyes fixed on the little chestnut horsehead at the end of the neck.

Adam lifted the instrument and placed it gently on his lap. His fingers instinctively stroked the mane of the little horse. A tiny white diamond-piece of wood had been skillfully inset into its forehead, between the eyes. Grandfather called him "Little Jabari." The name came from a real horse that he had loved and looked after when he was a boy, a chestnut stallion with a white diamond mark between the eyes. But that was in the Time Before. *They stole Jabari. They stole him . . . and our peace.* Grandfather said it hurt him to tell the story. He preferred to play his music. But even when his tunes were joyful, a dark shadow was never far behind. He always left it to Grandma to speak of that time.

Adam's fingers were curled around Little Jabari when he became aware of Grandma's hand on his shoulder. He hadn't heard her coming from the bedroom. It was usually in school that he got caught daydreaming.

"Oh, Grandma, you're so quiet! Where are Mama and Leila?" he asked, startled. "Mama said I must be back by lunch."

"They went to the market. Many people must be asking if your uncle got safely to the airport." Grandma limped around the settee and Adam felt the seat sink beside him.

"But I'm happy that you're here," she said. "Your uncle is right. We must think of you now as the man of the house. I know you will make us all proud, and your father"—Grandma's voice trembled for a moment before steadying—"would have been so proud to see you grow."

Adam frowned. He stared at the violin on his lap as words tried to form themselves.

"Grandma, can I ask you something about Grandfather and . . . and Dad?" As soon as he'd begun, he regretted it. This was something that he should have asked his father, not Grandma! The pain of the word *Dad* hovered between them. But Grandma quietly nodded. Adam felt the timpani drums in his heart starting up again.

"Did Dad think Grandfather should have done more to stop the Permitteds . . ." Adam's fingers stiffened around the horsehead scroll in his left palm. ". . . instead of spending so much time with his violin? Is that why they quarreled?"

Grandma remained silent for a while until, stretching out her wrinkled fingers, she took hold of his free hand.

"When your father was older, he learned that there are different ways to protest." Adam felt his grandmother's fingers pressing. "Your father wanted you to have this violin, Adam. He was just waiting for the right time."

Adam fastened his eyes on the little wooden horsehead, desperate not to cry. Even though Dad had never played the violin himself, he had made sure that his children attended music school. Grandfather's violin was Dad's final gift. He made himself look up at his grandmother.

"Grandma, tell me the story again of Jabari, the real one . . . and this one." He had heard it before. But never when it was just the two of them and when everything had become even harder to understand.

Grandma's hand tightened slightly around his palm as her eyes shifted inward . . .

My father bred horses. In fact, he was famous. People came from far away to our village to buy his horses. When he made some money, he was able to buy more land in our valley so we could grow many vegetables and fruit. A man from a nearby village came nearly every week over the hill with his donkey and cart to take our baskets of produce to sell in the Stone City. He was a Permitted, not a Non. We children called him Uncle Yosef.

Now, Uncle Yosef always came with his violin—this same violin that he had made himself. He would leave it inside our house early in the morning until he came back later in the afternoon. He and Father would first settle their business, then my mother would insist that he eat with us. Ummi loved to feed people! Uncle Yosef also loved horses. In fact, when Jabari was born, Father and Uncle Yosef agreed on his name together. Uncle Yosef said he had heard it from a man who traveled the world and that it meant valiant *or* fearless. *Father immediately liked it and was sure the chestnut foal would live up to his name.*

After dinner, the two men would play music together, Father with his oud and Uncle Yosef with his violin. In those days we didn't have such a big difference between Nons and Permitteds—and the OverPower ruled all of us. Father often listened to the radio. He told us that terrible things were happening to Uncle Yosef's people OverSeas. Father said that's why many wanted to escape and come here. The trouble started when some Permitted leaders claimed that our land belonged only to them and that everyone else, who had lived here for so many generations, didn't matter.

But Uncle Yosef wasn't like that. His family had also lived here for a long time. He spoke our language. He brought us children sweets and my mother often said to him, "You're spoiling the children!" But she never stopped him.

One day, I asked Ummi why he always went back to his home so late. "Doesn't Uncle Yosef have a wife and children of his own?"

My mother told us a sad story. Once, Uncle Yosef had a young wife. She was expecting their first child, but the baby came too early. The neighbors in his village rushed to bring help but by the time the midwife came, their baby, a son, had arrived. Dead. The poor mother had a raging fever herself and died just a few hours later. Ummi said Uncle Yosef blamed himself for not renting somewhere close to the city hospital before the baby was due. He said she was the only woman he had ever loved. He still dreamed of her.

"Since then, he shared his heart only with his violin," added Ummi.

When Grandma told this story, she usually stopped at this point. She sat silently for a little with her head bowed. Adam knew why. She was gathering the strength she needed for the next part of the story. . . .

In those days, in the Time Before, we shared a lot in our village. We helped each other, like good neighbors should. Now your grandfather, Tomas—although he wasn't your grandfather yet—was the son of one of our neighbors. He had only sisters, so he liked to come to our house to visit my brothers. Sometimes Tomas's father would be very cross that his son hadn't properly finished his work. It was usually something to do with the sheep. In the countryside, children have to work very hard, and they miss a lot of school, especially girls. In fact, I was lucky that our parents wanted me to go to school like my brothers.

Now, because Tomas was the only boy in his family, his parents expected him to do more. He was also a dreamer. This was something I always liked about him! He was different from most of the other boys, even my brothers. Often his father would come to our house and complain. Tomas this and Tomas that. Of course my father didn't want to offend his neighbor, but in truth he liked Tomas, especially because he was very good with Father's horses. When Tomas talked with a horse, it was like the animal understood him. He even got on with Uncle Yosef's donkey, and that donkey was really bad-tempered.

But that wasn't all. If he got the chance, Tomas liked to visit us when Father and Uncle Yosef played music together. Tomas would sway to the music and his head would nod. He was always fascinated by how the bow made the violin sing. Maybe that was because Uncle Yosef told us how only special horse hairs should be used to make a violin's bow. He also told us that his violin was special because of the horse-head he had carved at the end of the long wooden neck. Most violins, he said, had a curled scroll. The wood was the same chestnut color of Father's prize stallion. The carved horse-head even looked a bit like Father's Jabari, and that's how we gave it the nickname Little Jabari!

Uncle Yosef began to teach Tomas on his violin. We children used to laugh when the bow made scratches and squeaks, but Uncle Yosef was very patient and praised Tomas for his persistence. "You won't laugh for long," Uncle Yosef admonished us. "Tomas is a young man with courage." I remember him saying that, and he was right. Your grand-father soon began to play tunes we could all enjoy. Later, he would also show his courage in other ways.

Well, all this time, the news in our village, and on Father's radio, was becoming worse. The tension grew between us Nons and those Permitteds who wanted the OverPower to give the land just to them. Of course, we Nons protested. It was unfair. It was unjust. What would happen to us? People began fighting and being killed on each side. But Uncle Yosef kept coming with his cart and his violin, even when Father told him that it was getting too dangerous and he should stop coming. Everyone in our village knew him as someone who was helpful and friendly, but in times like this, anything could happen.

Then one morning, Uncle Yosef arrived on his cart looking very troubled. In the night, someone had painted the word Traitor on his door. His neighbors said they didn't know who'd done this, but they warned him not to come again to our village. He told Father that he didn't like to give in to threats. They talked and talked. In the end, Uncle Yosef agreed that he wouldn't come again until things had settled. I won't forget how he hugged each one of us children and, when he came to say goodbye to Ummi, he kept saying, "I'm so sorry, I'm so sorry." Then he went to his cart and lifted out his violin case. I was nearest to him and he pressed it into my arms. "Give this to Tomas. Tell him I shall make another violin. One day I hope that we shall play together." Then he climbed onto his cart, clutched the donkey's reins, and set *off. He turned his face away. I think he didn't want us to see his tears. We never saw him again.*

A few days later, we heard that a Non village near us had been attacked. Women, children, old people killed like animals. It was terrifying. We couldn't believe that such an inhuman thing could happen. Suddenly there was panic. People said we had to run to save our lives—leave straight away—or the same could happen to us. But no one wanted to leave their homes, their fields, and their animals. My father was crying, "Who will feed my horses?" My mother was also crying, "If we stay and they kill us, how will you feed your horses?"

So, my father harnessed Jabari and threw my mother's favorite carpet over his back. We filled up two sacks, one each side of Jabari, with kitchen things and a few clothes. Tomas helped to harness and lead my father's second stallion with two sacks of his family's possessions on its back. My older brother, Dawoud, took the best mare, loaded with blankets and a sack with barley, another with wheat and another with jars of Ummi's olive oil and preserved fruit. Ummi wanted to take more but Father insisted she stop. We followed on foot behind the three horses. At the last minute, I grabbed Uncle Yosef's violin, which was still in our house. I wrapped up the case in a bundle of clothes and carried it with me.

My father was distraught about the horses he had to leave

behind. He left the gate open so they could go looking for food in the hills. They knew something was wrong. We heard them neighing and whinnying as we hurried away. Other families left behind sheep, goats, hens . . . and came with nothing, nothing, only their lives. We all hoped to return home when the danger had passed. But we were wrong.

Grandma released Adam's hand—she had held it all this time—and he looked up to see Mama and Leila standing by the front door. His mother's eyes traveled between Grandma and the violin. Something in Mama's gaze told him she already knew about the gift. She had delayed coming back to give Grandma time with him alone.

"Come," said Mama quietly. "Let's have some lunch, then you two children must prepare for school tomorrow. You'll have a lot to make up." Leila came up close to Adam and pulled a face that only he could see, as if asking, *What was that with you and Grandma?* He was grateful for Mama's instruction to put Grandfather's violin in his room, giving him a few minutes alone.

"It's a long time since it was played," Mama added. "We'll need to get it checked." Mama made everything seem so matter-of-fact. How did she manage it? Adam's head was full of people fleeing. Great-grandfather distraught at leaving behind most of his horses. Grandma's mother crying. Uncle Yosef thrusting the violin case into young Grandma's hands, then turning away to hide his face. The same case he was now carrying to his bedroom with the same violin, Grandfather's, Uncle Yosef's. Maybe Uncle Yosef gave this gift to Grandfather because he knew what was happening was wrong, but he couldn't stop it.

Adam slipped the old violin case next to his much newer violin case beneath his desk. What were Uncle Yosef's last words? *Give this to Tomas. Tell him I shall make another violin. One day I hope that we shall play together.*

That had never happened. Most Permitteds that Adam saw were police or soldiers carrying guns, not violins. What good was a violin against a gun? Grandma hadn't given a straight answer to his question about Dad, as a young man, arguing with Grandfather. Instead, she had told him that Dad wanted him to have the old violin, and had just been waiting for the right time.

He knew her words were meant to comfort him, but there could never be a "right time" . . . not now that Dad had died.

IN OUR HOUSE

Dad's shadow

is everywhere . . .

and nowhere.

MR. B

IN THE MORNING, JUST AFTER breakfast, Zak popped his head around the door. Adam glimpsed the skateboard under his arm.

"I'll see you outside music school!" Zak grinned at Adam and Leila in their school uniforms before he disappeared. The shopkeeper, for whom Zak did odd jobs, let him leave the skateboard in his store while he was in school. It wasn't far from the park, and when Zak wasn't working, he would come to meet Adam and Leila after their music lessons. Their journey home was usually lively.

Mama poured herself a second cup of coffee as the children pulled on their backpacks.

"You'll walk with Leila all the way?"

Adam detected the anxiety in Mama's voice and nodded.

"You'll pick her up after school and go together to music school, won't you?"

Adam nodded again. Dad always used to walk with them before catching his bus to work. He would hold Leila's hand until they reached her school gate. Adam had long ago stopped letting his father hold his hand in public. But he had enjoyed having Dad to himself for a few minutes after leaving Leila. Sometimes they would talk or just keep in step with each other until they reached his school.

"Come on, Adam! We need to go!" Leila was getting impatient. He hadn't moved from the spot where he'd put on his backpack. He wanted to shout, "Leave me alone!" but a glance at his sister's washed-out face stopped him. Had she been crying last night? If so, she was making an effort to put on a brave face. He must do the same.

"Don't worry, Mama. We'll be okay," Leila said with a determined nod.

"Yes, we'll be okay," he repeated, trying to make his voice sound firm.

"It will be your first day back at music school and I'd really like to accompany you," said Mama. "But I need to see the lawyer and it's the only time he has today." She sounded apologetic.

"What for, Mama?" Leila cocked her head. Adam admired how his sister could be so direct.

"He needs me to explain something in the papers that he copied." Her eyes traveled to the red shoebox on top of

Dad's bookcase. "Your father was always very careful with the documents so there shouldn't be a problem." She was saying that to reassure them, thought Adam. But nothing about the red shoebox and Mama's permit had ever felt reassuring. This was Mama putting on her own brave face.

Adam felt self-conscious with Mama watching from the doorway as he and Leila descended the stone steps outside the house, his sister with her flute case and him with his violin case. They waved goodbye at the bottom. If his mother had X-ray eyes, she would see that Grandfather's violin was inside his case. He wanted to show it as soon as possible to Mr. B at music school. If he was going to be the man of the house, surely there were some decisions he could make on his own? He hoped Mr. B would find the old violin and bow in good condition, without needing any major repairs. Then he would tell Grandma and Mama, and it would save his mother the trouble when she had enough to worry about already.

Adam and Leila headed toward the Northwest Gate in silence. It was the way they always used to walk with Dad in the morning, past the old mission school building, which towered over the stone-cobbled road. How many times had Dad told them that, seventy years ago, Grandma and Grandfather Tomas had managed to get work here in the school kitchen? *Just think what that must have been like for your grandma. Before, her father could have sent her to that school. Afterward, she was lucky to get a job in the kitchen.*

Leila stayed close to Adam as they crossed the main road outside the gate. Was his usually chatty, bouncy sister also battling with memories? He didn't want to ask. He was having trouble dealing with his own. The main road was noisier as they made their way among people on their way to work. Dad's favorite route took them past his friend's bookshop so they could exchange a few words. If Uncle Mikhail was busy with a customer at the front counter, he would wave to them. His shop was around the corner from music school and had a café. On the weekend, when the children had orchestra practice, Dad would go there to find new books, drink coffee, and talk. When Adam and Leila went there afterward, Uncle Mikhail always gave them juice and cake.

Today, Adam chose a different, shorter route. Although he didn't say anything, he wondered whether his sister was also worried about returning to school. Some school friends had come with their families to offer condolences at home, but he was expecting awkward glances from others. At the entrance to Leila's building, instead of giving her regular wave, she hesitated, looking forlorn.

"I'll come straight after school," he promised before hurrying on to his own school.

The yard was bustling before the bell, but as soon as a few students and teachers came to say how sorry they were to hear about his father, he began to feel less tense. Indeed, some of the things people said left him feeling proud. Some students passed on what their parents had said. A few words circulated in his brain . . . *important . . . truth . . . steadfast.* He hadn't realized how many people knew of Dad's work as an archaeologist.

When his history teacher announced within everyone's hearing, "We Nons shall always be grateful to your father, Adam, for looking after our history," he suddenly felt overwhelmed. He squeezed back tears by staring down at his violin case. If he could just take out Grandfather's violin and play, he could forget everyone and everything. His tangled feelings would dissolve in the music. That would be so much easier than attempting any words.

After school, Leila was waiting where he had left her. She hurried toward him, her flute case knocking against her leg. He wanted to ask about her day, but as soon as their eyes met, he knew she too had been struggling. Instead, they kept a brisk pace until they reached the wrought-iron gates of their music school.

Closing the gate behind them shut out the busy street. They were early and the courtyard was calm. Leafy shadows from lofty eucalyptus trees danced over the black-and-white patterns of the marble paving stones. The stone harp in the middle of the courtyard and the arched doorway of the grand limestone house invited them into another world. This had once been the home of a respected Non family. Inside, the high ceilings and elegant staircase came from the Time Before.

The receptionist said that Mr. B was already in his room. His teacher's real name was long, and everyone called him Mr. B or Mr. Bellissimo. Mr. B was a fine violinist and insisted on his students repeating notes or phrases, even whole pieces of music, until he would call out, "Bellissimo!" They all knew that Mr. B insisted on music being beautiful. *You're just like Mr. B!* Adam had said that more than once to his father when Dad had insisted on him doing better.

With a wave to Leila, Adam hurried up the stairs. Mr. B's door was open. Stepping inside without even knocking, Adam placed his case on the nearest chair.

"Please, sir!" Adam opened the clasps and lifted the old violin. "This was my grandfather's, Mr. B. It hasn't been played since he died."

If Mr. B was surprised, he didn't show it as he took the instrument. Carefully and methodically, he examined it. Finally, he turned his attention to Little Jabari.

"Bellissimo!" he murmured, admiring the carving of the mane, the pricked-up ears, the nostrils, and the tiny white diamond shape in the forehead. "So unusual . . . and it looks in good condition." He picked up the bow and, after adjusting the bow hairs, he rubbed on a generous amount of rosin.

"Let's hear you, my friend," Mr. B said, almost tenderly, lifting the violin again. His left forefinger and thumb, gently yet firmly, began turning each peg. With the bow sweeping upward, he tested each string until he was happy with the sound. He did it by ear, without even a tuning fork. Just like Grandfather before he became too frail.

"We should replace these old strings, but first let's hear the instrument as it is." Mr. B held out the violin.

Adam hesitated. He hadn't been practicing. "Please, sir, will you try it first?"

Mr. B raised his bushy black eyebrows while tucking the violin under his chin. The bow began to draw out slow mournful notes and Adam recognized an old Non melody. Gradually the pace increased until a strong, urgent rhythm emerged. Adam felt his foot begin to tap, but suddenly Mr. B stopped.

"Let's try something else now . . . to remind us of springtime and new life. You'll remember this from last year's concert, Adam. A grade eight played it. As you know, Vivaldi is one of my favorites."

This time Mr. B let the bow dance lightly over the strings. Birds were singing in olive trees overflowing with white blossoms! Like those on the remaining piece of hillside outside the city where Dad took the family to picnic at the beginning of every summer. Soon Adam was imagining the real Jabari flying with Grandfather as a boy—flying freely together across a wide-open hillside, through fields of yellow buttercups and red poppies, leaping over streams in the valley—until Mr. B lifted up the bow and Adam returned to earth in front of his music teacher.

"An excellent violin, Adam. Where did your grandfather acquire it?"

"It's a long story, sir." How much did he want to share? Yet Mr. B had just made his violin sing so he felt he was flying. "My grandma's father had a friend who made it himself." Adam paused. "He was a Permitted, sir."

"So . . . a special violin with a special story . . ." Mr. B fell silent. Adam watched his teacher's finger stroke Little Jabari's mane.

"Yes, it comes from the Time Before, sir." Adam wanted to move on. "Will you teach me on this violin, sir?"

"Absolutely!" Mr. B's voice rose whenever he was pleased or excited. He held out the violin and bow. "But you will only do this beautiful instrument justice if you practice, practice, practice!"

"Thank you, Mr. B!" A bubble of nervousness threatened to burst through Adam's lips as he tucked the violin under his chin. It was a few months still to the summer concert. Could he become good enough to perform with Little Jabari there? Sometimes there were even special visitors. He could make Grandma and Mama so proud! He pushed away any thought of Mama losing her permit . . . and that Dad wouldn't be there.

INTRUDERS IN THE ALLEY

LEILA WAS CHATTING WITH SOME girls by the stone harp when Adam entered the courtyard and made straight for the gate. With a quick wave to her friends, she caught up with him.

"Why such a hurry?" Her high ponytails were still swinging on either side of her head.

"Mama and Grandma will be waiting for us."

Leila looked at him curiously but didn't probe any further. Outside the gate, there was no sign of Zak with his skateboard.

"Shall we go by the park?" asked Leila. She seemed in better spirits than before music school.

"Not today." Adam didn't add that, if Zak were there, he didn't want to go skateboarding. Not even now that he was feeling more confident of his balance. He just wanted to get Grandfather's violin home and explain how he had taken it to show Mr. B. Mama and Grandma would surely be pleased that it didn't need any major repairs.

A noisy green tractor came hurtling out of the Great Gate just as they reached the entrance. The driver and two men standing in its trailer grinned as pedestrians hurried out of the way. Adam and Leila squeezed their backs against the police railings.

Once the tractor had gone, they made their way with the afternoon crowds between stalls with plastic toys, children's shoes, coloring books, sweets, cell phones, rolls of material for dresses and curtains, ornaments, spices, and fresh fruit and vegetables. Turning off the main thoroughfare, the children began climbing the wide stone steps that Zak loved leaping down on his skateboard. It always amazed Adam that the merchants sitting on plastic chairs outside their shops, on different levels of the steps, never shouted at him seriously. Sometimes Zak scraped past closer than a buzz cut! Yet he had never crashed into the merchandise, let alone a person. Occasionally, someone would even call out praise for his skill. Only tourists sometimes seemed a little startled, and Zak was smart enough never to go near Permitted police on patrol.

This afternoon there was no sign of Zak here in the market area, carrying out errands on his skateboard. It was over a couple of weeks since they had walked this way, and they found the next street was already decorated with early Easter flags. While not as steep, this street had no shops and was quieter, especially as Zak wasn't skimming up against the stone walls on either side, making a great big clatter. He liked to leap up under the flying arches, touching the arches with his outstretched fingertips.

Today, however, Adam and Leila were wrapped in their own thoughts until a pair of Permitted police suddenly loomed up ahead. Leila placed a hand on Adam's shoulder. He felt her unease. The officers stood at the entrance to the alley that was the shortest way home, the one with the little yellow parakeet. Although their rifles pointed down, the officers' fingers remained on the triggers. Adam and Leila stopped.

"We live down there," said Adam, trying to see into the alley. He expected to be waved away with a flick of the hand. Instead, four police eyes scanned them, pausing on the violin and flute cases. The officers glanced at each other. Then, unexpectedly, one stood back and signaled with a finger that the children could enter. The space was only enough for one at a time. Adam stepped forward, steadying his breath, checking over his shoulder for his sister.

With the Permitted police now behind them, Adam could hear their father's voice. *Don't run.* His heart was beating faster but they walked on as calmly as they could, side by side. This was not the time to stop and talk to the parakeet. This end of the alley was strangely quiet with no one else in sight. However, voices grew louder as they drew near the bend in the alley . . . angry Non voices. As soon as they turned the corner, it was clear what was happening. A large pile of furniture, carpets, bedding, and pots and pans had been roughly thrown up near the door to the last house on the right.

"Those belong to Zak's aunty Hala!" Leila exclaimed. The green-velvet settee from her sitting room formed part of a barricade where Permitted police were guarding a slim exit into the road. Permitteds must have taken Aunt Hala's house! On the far side of the barricade, people were shouting. Yet the neighboring houses were strangely quiet. Any protestors inside the alley must already have been forced out.

"It's a trap!" Leila gripped Adam's arm.

"We have to go on." He did his best to hold his voice on a firm note. This eviction was what Zak's father and Dad had been trying to stop by going to court all those times.

As they drew closer to Aunt Hala's house, a large man in a white shirt and black trousers suddenly appeared at her door. His bushy beard was similar to Uncle Musa's, but he was taller and broader than Zak's father.

"Who are you?" he demanded, stepping out in front of them. Without waiting for a reply, he pointed to their instrument cases. "What's inside?"

The man's gestures were clear, and Adam knew enough Permitted language to understand. "We live here!" he retorted in Non, raising his chin.

"Around the corner," confirmed Leila, her voice higher than usual. "We come home this way after music school."

"You could have stones in there. Let me see!" Without warning, the man lunged toward Adam to grab the violin case. Fearing it would break open and Grandfather's violin would crash to the ground, Adam let go.

He watched the stubby fingers push open each catch and lift the lid. The man's eyes rested briefly on the violin before shifting back to Adam.

"What's a Non boy like you doing with a beautiful violin like this?" The voice was lower now but Adam heard the menace. Why did he have to tell this Permitted man anything about the violin made by his great-grandfather's friend Uncle Yosef? The man might even claim it really belonged to a Permitted. Anyway, it was none of his business. Adam threw Leila a look to say *Don't answer*, but his heart was thumping. What if the man just took it? A woman police officer, standing on this side of the exit, casually observed them but said nothing.

With the open case in his arms, the man turned and called into the house. "Come and see this, son!" A boy who looked only a little older than Adam, dressed like his father but slimmer, appeared in the doorway. He had close-cut, sand-colored hair, and he gazed suspiciously at Adam through his pale blue eyes.

At the same moment came a high-pitched scream of "Stop, thief!" as two stones, in sharp succession, twanged against a pan at the top of the furniture pile. The voice was Zak's! Glancing upward, Adam glimpsed a head bob behind a water tank on the rooftop opposite the end of the alley.

The intruder man swung around, his eyes like furious searchlights. The woman police officer walked swiftly toward him. She was replaced by another officer at the exit.

"What's the problem here?"

"Can't you see?" he snapped. "This boy's friends are threatening me with stones!"

"What's this about?" She pointed to the violin. Adam was sure she had heard everything, but she was giving the man a chance to explain.

"You said no one would be allowed in until we finished moving in!" His voice rose. "I was just checking the case for stones."

The policewoman stayed unruffled. "Don't worry, we'll see to the others. Let these two go."

"Hmmmh!" A rumble came from the man's throat as he slammed the violin case shut and thrust it toward Adam. The policewoman said nothing to the children but signaled for them to go. She called to the officer at the exit to let them out.

From the other side of Aunt Hala's green settee and the barricade, Non voices were now shouting, "Stop the thieves! Stop the thieves!"

Adam's eyes met Leila's. They were fiery but he saw the streak of fear. Had she also spotted Zak behind the water tank? What if the Permitteds caught him? Leila knew now about Grandfather's violin inside the case . . . and how close it had come to being seized. The announcement he had planned for Mama and Grandma was now messed up. So was everything else.

AVALANCHE

OUTSIDE IN THE ROAD, AUNT Hala wiped her tears with the corner of her headscarf while demanding that the police let her back into the alley. Uncle Musa, with his phone to his ear, barely glanced at the children as they began to weave through the throng of people. Zak was nowhere to be seen.

When they reached Uncle Musa's house, the door was open. Loud voices and crying came from inside. Suddenly there was Mama in the doorway, holding Aunt Hala's twins by the hand, a five-year-old on each side. "I said you'll play with these little ones for a couple of hours while things are being sorted out."

Adam and Leila had often laughed at the twins' antics when they pretended to imitate Zak on his skateboard. But today, their usually sparkling eyes were dull and flat. They would have been at home with their mother when the Permitted family broke in.

They found Grandma on the settee with her embroidery. Her face revealed that she already knew what had happened to their neighbors. She laid down her needlework and held out her arms to the little boys. They let her hug them but stood listless. Not even Grandma's special tin of sweets, which Leila brought from the cupboard, got a response. Each boy took a sweet and ate it without any change in expression. It was the same when Mama called the children to the table for orange juice and cookies. Afterward, when Leila brought out crayons and paper for drawing, neither twin responded.

"Maybe later," Grandma murmured. Leila gave up and joined Mama, who was spreading out vegetables on the kitchen counter.

"You can help me chop these, Leila. We'll make a big pot of lentil stew and take it across to Zak's family." At the mention of Zak's name, the twins turned to look at Mama but said nothing, their faces still blank.

Adam remained sitting at the table. If Leila hadn't managed to distract the twins, how could he? He was wondering how he could slip away to his bedroom when Grandma made a request.

"Adam, play something for us, please." She was looking at his violin case. Ordinarily, he would have taken it straight to his room, but today he and Leila had deposited their backpacks and instrument cases beside the front door. If he opened his case here, Grandma and Mama would see that it contained Grandfather's violin! His plan to tell them first the good news from Mr. B was in a mess.

"I—I need to put some more rosin on the bow, Grandma . . ." He faltered. "Then I'll come and play for you." He hurried to pick up his case and remove it to his bedroom.

But Grandma patted the settee beside her. "Do it here, Adam, so the twins can see."

His heart sank but he walked to the settee and sat down with the case. A jumble of words revolved in his mind while Grandma signaled to Zak's young cousins to come. Silently, they obeyed and once again she pulled the small boys close to her.

"Shall we help Adam open his case? What can be inside?" Grandma's soft voice was so inviting that both twins stretched out their fingers to help lift the clasps and lid.

In the alley, Adam had felt dread when the Permitted man opened his case. Now, as Grandma's and Mama's gazes transferred from Grandfather's violin to his face, he felt hot with shame. His parents had always insisted on honesty, and of course he should have asked Mama before taking it out of the house! Her raised eyebrows showed disapproval. At least Grandma didn't look cross, only quizzical.

"Mr. B says Grandfather's violin is in very good condition for its age." His words tumbled out. "He says the strings can be changed but it sounds fine. Shall I show you?"

"Go ahead, Adam." Mama's tone indicated that this wasn't the end of the matter. She just didn't want an argument in front of the twins, who were both peering at Little Jabari.

Adam elevated the violin so the small chestnut horse was at their eye level. Leila came over from the kitchen. "You can stroke him!" she said, running her finger down the wooden mane. After a moment's hesitation, the boys copied her.

Adam began to feel a little calmer. His sister hadn't said anything about what had nearly happened to the violin in the alley. The music would also help him think more clearly. He would play a song that he had been learning with Mr. B as a surprise for Grandma. It was a song she loved, from a singer who always lifted people's spirits. He hadn't imagined playing it on an occasion like this.

Adam was aware of everyone's eyes on him as he raised Grandfather's violin into position. Grandma was still holding the twins while Leila knelt beside them. Mama remained by the kitchen counter, although no longer chopping vegetables.

"What about the rosin, Adam? You said the bow needed

some." Mama missed nothing. His rosin cake lay snugly at the bottom of the case, wrapped in its soft orange cloth.

"It will be all right, Mama. Mr. B rubbed it on before using the bow." His eyes met briefly with Mama's. At least he hadn't added another lie.

Checking his arm position and the violin for a second time, he took a few slow breaths and lifted his bow. Closing his eyes, he could hear the opening melody in his head. *We and the moon are neighbors* . . . But just as he was about to begin, Zak's father was at the door.

"Is Zak here?" Uncle Musa's voice was urgent. He fixed his eyes on Adam. "Have you seen him?"

"No, Uncle. He's not here." Adam recalled the head bobbing behind the water tank, the screams of "Stop, thief!" and stones striking Aunt Hala's pan on top of the furniture pile. What could he say without getting Zak into trouble? But before he could work it out, Leila spoke.

"Uncle, we heard a voice like Zak's near Aunt Hala's house, but we didn't see him." Had Leila not spotted Zak? Nor did she mention the stones. Yet what she said was true.

"I also heard him shouting, but I was busy contacting people to come and help us . . . and now he hasn't come home." Uncle Musa threw open his arms. His upturned palms seemed to beg like empty bowls. Adam's stomach tightened. The police would have been searching for the source of the stones.

Mama tried to be reassuring. "We know that he's an enterprising boy, Musa, and there's still time for him to get back before supper. We'll bring the food to your house as soon as it's ready." Then she changed tack. "I was thinking, how will you manage with so many people in your house? You know Zak can come and share Adam's room for a while."

It took Adam a couple of moments to take in Mama's offer. However much he enjoyed the crazy fun he had with Zak, sharing his room all the time would be something else. For one thing, he couldn't imagine practicing his violin with Zak there.

"We can also store some of your sister's belongings," Mama continued.

A picture of Aunt Hala's furniture suddenly merged in Adam's head with an image of a huge snow-covered mountain from his school project about avalanches. What was it Dad had said? *Imagine a sudden weight—even just a person's foot—landing on the snow where there's a weak area under the surface. That one foot, Adam, can trigger a massive avalanche that affects hundreds of others.*

Adam barely heard the rest of the conversation. Aunt Hala's eviction was like the first weight in an avalanche. Once Permitteds swept away one Non family from a section of the Stone City, they would look to sweep away the next . . . and the next . . . as Dad had predicted . . . Dad who was no longer here to help them resist. Missing Dad felt like a hole growing deeper inside him.

"Adam, we're waiting for you," Grandma said gently after Uncle Musa had left. Once again, he raised Grandfather's violin into position. He eyed Little Jabari while trying to bring the melody back into his head. When it came, Adam and his audience allowed themselves, for a few minutes, to forget the day's events.

MY NIGHTMARE

Family photographs
behind shattered glass,
a forest of chair legs
poke to the sky.
A jumble piled high
of upside-down beds,
Aunt Hala's curtains
ripped in shreds.
The mountain grows and grows,
suddenly smothered in snow.
Zak on skateboard—
speeding, swirling,
twisting, twirling.
Someone chasing,
Zak racing,
snow sliding,
colliding . . .
silence

NEEDED! A HORSE OF POWER!

UNCLE MUSA APPEARED WITH A stack of chairs as Adam and Leila were finishing breakfast. The bags under his eyes showed he hadn't slept.

"Zak?" Mama's question shot out even before a greeting.

"He came home after midnight, clothes torn. Said people were chasing him. I took him right away to my cousin's family outside the Stone City. They'll keep him safe."

"So sorry, so sorry!" Mama expressed her sympathy.

Adam could imagine Zak's protests. Even though it was for his own good, he was being banned from his own home! He would miss the demonstrations near Aunt Hala's house. Already there were sounds of shouting, drums, and whistles coming from down the road. The protestors were starting early.

"Does he have his skateboard, Uncle?" Leila asked. From her worried frown, Adam knew that they shared the same thought. For Zak not to have his skateboard would be harsh punishment . . . almost as bad as not being allowed home.

"No! No!" Uncle Musa waved his finger for emphasis. "He has to stay inside the house. Only the family should know."

"But Uncle, Zak didn't start the trouble—"

"That's enough, Adam!" Mama intervened. "Uncle Musa is tired. Take Aunty Hala's chairs and put them between your bed and your bookcase."

So much for being "the man of the house," thought Adam, as he collected the chairs.

After Uncle Musa had gone, Mama said the children must promise they would only use the Northwest Gate to and from school. "I don't want you anywhere near the protests, is that clear?"

Adam flinched at Mama's words. Surely Dad would have wanted them to support the demonstrators and Uncle Musa's family? Their protest was right! Mama was standing in front of the bookcase filled with Dad's books on archaeology and history, many about Non people. In fact, Adam had heard Dad call it his "protest bookcase" because so many Permitteds insisted that Nons had *no* history!

It was on the tip of Adam's tongue to object to such a

total ban when he spotted, on the top shelf, the red shoebox with the papers for Mama's permit application. He didn't need Mama to explain that you didn't have to do anything wrong at a demonstration to find yourself in trouble. Everyone knew about informers who pretended to be protestors. They reported on anyone who was there, including children. That could be enough to stop Mama receiving her permit. An unpleasant bitter taste suddenly filled Adam's mouth. Clamping his lips, he hurried to his bedroom to collect his schoolbag.

Mama came to the top of the stone steps to wave goodbye and watch the children turn in the direction of the Northwest Gate.

"I'll expect you back by three o'clock!" Mama called after them. They weren't going to music school today and Adam knew she'd keep checking the time until they were home.

Over the next few weeks, it became a pattern. Mama would watch Adam and Leila leave in the morning while Grandma was still in bed. When Dad was alive, Grandma had usually been the first to rise and put on the coffee. But since they had lost Dad and since Uncle Elias had left, she had become much slower and quieter. At Easter, the children even had to beg Grandma to make her delicious cookies. That had never happened before. This year, Mama, Adam, and Leila did most of the preparation, with Mama coaxing Grandma to comment on their efforts. For the first time, Grandma was too tired to come and watch the procession with the marchers, drums, and bright flags. She said she was reserving her energy for the Easter Sunday service.

Adam now realized that when Grandma sat telling him the story of Grandfather's violin, it must have taken a lot of effort. She had already gone through so much in her life and now, adding to her sad memories, this. The eviction of Aunt Hala—with family and possessions scattered, some into Grandma's own home—was, in Mama's words, "like having a scab pulled off an old wound."

The large crowd of demonstrators against the eviction had gradually dwindled to just a few protestors who continued to call in at Uncle Musa's house to show they hadn't forgotten. There were still two police officers at the end of the alley, and Uncle Musa insisted that Zak remain with his cousins. He should attend their school, at least until the end of the school year in June.

During the Easter holidays, Adam and Leila missed Zak more than ever. Whenever they asked Uncle Musa about Zak, he always just repeated, "Fine. He's fine." But everything had changed. There was no Zak, no roaming, and no chance of a bit of fun. Instead, there were only worried, anxious adults in both families . . . and Dad, with his steady, measured voice, was no longer there to say,

"We'll find a way." Without Zak, school, and homework to occupy chunks of Adam's time, the ache of Dad's absence increased over the holidays.

Adam thought it must be the same for Leila. She remained much quieter too, and when she wasn't helping Mama or Grandma, she would retreat to her bed with a book. Although she practiced her flute, especially when reminded by Mama, his sister didn't seem able to lose herself in the music like Adam did. Sometimes when he practiced, he could completely forget the time. Nevertheless, when the Easter holidays came to an end, it was a relief to return to school.

Problems, however, remained the same. Uncle Musa hadn't been able to find other accommodation for his sister's family inside the Stone City. When he said that he would have to look elsewhere, Zak's grandmother had cried. She was used to seeing Aunt Hala and her children every day. How would that be possible if they lived far away? Their family was being torn apart. Grandma lamented with her childhood friend, while Mama did her best to comfort Zak's mother over her absent son.

In their own family, there was no news from the lawyer dealing with Mama's permit. Mama's anxiety would often appear through a sharper-than-usual voice. "Is that all the homework you've got, Adam?" "Was that really your best flute practice, Leila?" "Shouldn't you practice more scales, Adam?"

In the past, Grandma might have intervened with a softening comment. Now, she listened mostly in silence.

Whenever he could, Adam slipped away to play Grandfather's violin in his bedroom. Thanks to his violin teacher, it now had a new set of strings, making it, in Mr. B's words, "even more bellissimo." Knowing the sound carried from his bedroom into the sitting room, Adam often ended his practice with one of the old Non melodies that Grandma loved so much. At least when his head was filled with music, everything else could fade away.

One evening, a couple of weeks after the new term started, Leila had gone to bed and Adam was still doing homework at the table when Grandma quietly asked Mama about going back to her choir. Mama had always loved singing, saying that it freed her mind. When she came back from choir singing or humming a tune, Dad used to say it was like a fresh breeze entering their house. Even though Mama made sure the children kept up their music practice, they hadn't heard her singing or humming for a couple of months now.

"I don't know," Mama muttered in reply to Grandma. "It's more difficult."

"You can leave the children with me," said Grandma. "It would do you good." Adam thought Grandma must be feeling a little better to make the offer.

"Not as much good, Mother, as knowing that I had a

permit for the next year—" Mama stopped, as if suddenly regretting her abruptness. "Let me think about it."

When Dad was alive, he had always been at home with them on choir evenings. Everything had been so different then. But what was the point of thinking about those times, Adam told himself fiercely, when they could never come back?

He found it hard to fall asleep that night. Mama had almost snapped at Grandma. She must be really anxious about her permit, however good the lawyer. It was too late now to play his violin. He took out the leather-bound book from Uncle Elias and reread the few poems he had written. The last was "Avalanche," and he hadn't written anything since the final word, "silence."

His poems just brought back the ache of missing Dad. But he also missed Zak with his skateboard and the crazy jokes that made him laugh. Surely Zak was missing him and Leila too? Everything had changed so much since Dad had died, and then Aunt Hala's eviction. Adam still felt guilty that when Mama had suggested Zak could share his bedroom, his first thought had been that it would interfere with his violin practice.

To stop his mind from churning, Adam opened his book of folktales from Dad and reread Dad's inscription, pausing on the sentence, *Maybe the people inside the stories are not all that different from us today with the same nightmares, dreams, and hopes . . .* Then, flicking over some pages, he stopped at an old favorite. It was also one of Dad's favorites. The opening words acted like a spell. . . .

Once upon a time a strong and powerful czar ruled a country far away, and among his servants was a young archer, and this archer had a horse—a horse of power—such a horse as belonged to the wonderful men of long ago. . . .

Swept into the story, Adam imagined the horse of power with a shining chestnut coat, flowing mane, flaring ears, and a white diamond patch on his forehead. Like the young archer, he was riding through the forest where birds no longer sang and where a golden feather lay on the path. Oh, how he wanted to pick it up, except his horse of power warned him . . .

"If you take it, you will be sorry for it, and know the meaning of fear."

But how could he not take it? *You'll be sorry if you do. Sorry if you don't.* Both fear and daring gripped the young archer! Yet whatever the terror ahead, his horse of power had a plan, so long as he was brave enough to carry it out.

Adam closed the book. Half awake, half dreaming, he

imagined a horse whinnying . . . like a huge impatient Jabari . . . outside their front door . . . calling him!

You need courage to face fear, Adam!

It was the kind of thing Dad would have said. He wanted to sleep but now felt too awake. He reached again for Uncle Elias's book and turned to the next blank page.

I MISS YOU, DAD

You loved stories, Dad . . .

I remember
you loved the horse of power
telling the young archer
in the Forest of Fear,
"You have to be brave!"

I remember
you sat on my bed and said,
"Find the truth in a story!
Tell it
and the truth stays alive."

I remember
you explained to Leila and me
that Permitteds could send Mama away
over the Wall
but you wouldn't let them.

I remember
I asked how can you stop them?
You said we must use our voices!
Permitteds love their families
and we love ours too.

I remember
you said Permitteds want to silence us
in their Forest of Fear!
That's why you loved
the wise horse of power.

I don't have a horse of power,
just Little Jabari,
Grandfather's violin,
and your voice in my head, saying,
"You have to be brave!"

I miss you, Dad, I miss you.

ADAM'S PLAN

NEXT DAY IN SCHOOL ADAM was scolded twice for not paying attention, first in math, then in history.

"It's not like you, Adam!" his history teacher chided. "You're usually one of the first to have something to say."

"Sorry, sir," he mumbled. Since waking, his mind had been tumbling with questions. What should he say to Mr. B, and would Mr. B agree? Would his idea seem crazy and . . . could he carry it off? He couldn't tell Mr. B his whole plan.

"Well, whatever you are thinking about, it's not the time for it now." His history teacher's voice was stern but not unkind. It was a tone Dad might have used. Although Adam did his best to concentrate on the rest of his lessons, he kept checking his watch until the end-of-school bell.

Adam saw the flatness in Leila's eyes when he met her outside her school. Did she also sometimes feel a sudden wave of emptiness while surrounded by other people? But he didn't ask. He was just about managing himself, and now he needed all his energy for his plan. Instead, he increased his pace as they walked to music school.

"We're *not* late!" Leila protested.

Adam didn't explain that he needed extra time with Mr. B. Nor did he slow down, although he was becoming less sure of what he was going to say. Mr. B had come to Dad's funeral, but it wasn't like he was a family friend who knew them well. Yet Adam was going to speak about how their mother would be deported over the Wall if she didn't get her permit. He hadn't even discussed his idea with Mama herself, even though it was all about her! However, if Mama were deported, that would affect them all. There would definitely be no more lessons at music school.

Last night, in bed, anything seemed possible. Hurrying now beside cars, scooters, and pedestrians, Adam tightened his grip on his violin case. If only Little Jabari could really become a horse of power, what would he advise? A driver honked.

You'll be sorry if you do. Sorry if you don't.

Crossing the marble courtyard beneath the eucalyptus trees, Adam felt the change of tempo from the street. The old limestone building, with its high ceilings and arches, was instantly calming. He should apologize to Leila for rushing, but she had already peeled away from him to join some girls. Inside, he measured his steps up the grand staircase, letting his breath become steady and his head clear.

There was really only one thing he needed to ask Mr. B. It wasn't necessary to tell him the whole story about Mama. Nor did he need to reveal his entire plan. All he needed was for Mr. B to teach him Vivaldi's "Spring" in time for the summer concert. It need only be the first movement. That would be enough.

Mr. B was sitting at his desk when Adam made his request. The bushy black eyebrows came closer together as he frowned. "Do you really think you can learn this so quickly, Adam? It's a higher grade, and I don't want your other work to suffer."

"But I want to try, Mr. B!" Adam pleaded. "I'll do extra practice, I promise! I've loved it, Mr. B, ever since I first heard it. It makes me think of my grandma's stories from the Time Before. My grandfather rode horses in the valley with a stream . . . and over hills. The music takes me there, Mr. B . . . and then you played it on Grandfather's violin! I love it so much and so will—" He stopped himself just in time. Little Jabari was his secret. He didn't want Mr. B, or anyone else, thinking he was crazy to talk about the wooden horsehead as if it were real.

Mr. B was silent for a few moments. What he said next made Adam's heart skip a beat. "Well, I think I can tell you, Adam, that our next concert won't be an ordinary one. A famous violinist will come from OverSeas to work with our young musicians. We don't want this widely known as yet, so I trust you to keep this to yourself. You will be taking on a very big challenge. I'll only let you do it if you're ready. Agreed?"

Adam's lips moved, his voice barely a whisper. "Yes, Mr. B!" As he lifted the violin in order to tune it, he felt light-headed. He hadn't said anything about Mama's situation, nor about what he intended to say to the audience after their applause. He just had to dazzle them first with Vivaldi's "Spring"! If he could do that, he could imagine the headline: FUTURE OF PROMISING YOUNG NON MUSICIAN UNDER THREAT. The world-famous musician would say what a tragedy it would be to lose young talent and, when Adam was interviewed, he would say what deporting Mama would do to their family and how unjust it was to separate families. He would also speak about his violin and its story, starting with Uncle Yosef and Great-Grandfather.

"Adam?" Mr. B's voice brought him back to reality. "We have no time to lose! You need to practice, practice, practice!"

Glancing briefly toward Little Jabari before lowering his eyes, Adam raised his bow and began.

That night, as soon as Adam put his head on his pillow, Mr. B's words raced around his mind. In the end, there was only one way to put them to rest. He climbed out of bed and took out Uncle Elias's book.

HOW HIGH CAN A HEART FLY?

My heart flies
higher than the eucalyptus trees.
Mr. B has agreed!
He's the strictest teacher ever!
Even if I practice all day
he'll find something I need to do better.
Mr. B's words replay
in my head.
Bold echoes
beat on a drum.
A famous violinist
will come from OverSeas
to work with young musicians.
Practice, practice, practice
every spare minute!

PRACTICE, PRACTICE, PRACTICE

"WE HARDLY SEE YOU THESE days, Adam, now that you're so busy with your new pieces!" Mama gave Adam a quick smile as he sat down for dinner, but there was also something else in her voice.

"I've already told you, Mama. It's the first time I'll be playing Grandfather's violin in public—but only if Mr. B says it's 'Bellissimo!'"

"I'm glad my flute teacher isn't as strict as your Mr. B!" Leila's eyebrows rose like two question marks as she whistled a few notes from his Vivaldi piece. Adam was stopped from retorting by Grandma.

"Your grandfather would have liked that music." Grandma's gray head was bent over her plate and her voice was barely above a whisper. "He would have liked Uncle Yosef to go on teaching him. He was a very good teacher . . . just like your Mr. B . . . until . . ."

Mama's hand rested on the serving spoon. She allowed time for Grandma's words and the silence that followed to sink in before she began dishing out rice. "And you, Leila, could do with copying your brother's example to do your very best . . ."

It was Adam's turn to grin.

". . . while you're still able to attend music school."

His smile faded.

The children now came home earlier after school. They no longer called in at Uncle Mikhail's bookshop, where they used to love browsing in the children's section. "You must look at this!" he would say, holding up new books he thought they'd enjoy, which Dad would buy for them later. This was always after Dad and Uncle Mikhail had finished discussing events from the Stone City to the other side of the world. Even when the events were terrible, as they often were, it was always reassuring to hear their voices in the background. These days just walking near the bookshop brought a wave of misery over Adam. He could tell that Leila felt it too, although neither of them said anything. The memories were too painful.

But all that time was gone now, and Mama expected them home within half an hour. After music school, there also were no more diversions to the park with Zak on his skateboard. Mama continued to insist that they avoid the Great Gate and the alleys where Permitteds hung their flags out of windows in houses taken from Nons. They could no longer stop and talk to the little yellow parakeet.

Adam spent more time in his room, alone with his violin. Practicing his scales and Vivaldi's "Spring" took his mind far away. His right arm and bow were becoming swifter and lighter, his left fingers more nimble and sure. At times, he could even begin to imagine himself flying over hills with his Jabari.

"Excellent progress!" Mr. B was pleased. It wasn't quite "Bellissimo!" but Adam beamed at the praise. "Keep up this progress, young man, and you'll have your audience dreaming of a valley in spring . . . birds in the trees above and a little stream below!"

Mr. B was already talking as though he would be allowed to play the Vivaldi at the concert! Adam wanted to pinch himself. He just had to keep up his practice and keep improving. As long as Mama wasn't refused her permit *before* the concert! It would be much more difficult to change a decision that was already made. But if he could get attention and publicity beforehand, maybe—just maybe—the Permitteds would decide to let Mama stay.

As he packed Grandfather's violin away in his case after Mr. B's praise, Adam winked at his secret ally, Little Jabari.

UP IN THE AIR

AS ADAM SHUT THE IRON gate behind Leila, a sharp whistle cut the air. A second later, Zak leaped out from behind the wall on his skateboard.

"Hey, Adam! Hey, Leila!" he called with a wide grin. Spinning around at the corner, he landed with a clatter beside them before jumping off the deck, as softly as a cat onto the pavement. He burst into laughter at their amazed looks.

"Did your dad say you can come here?" Leila's question popped out at the same time as Adam's "So you got your skateboard back!"

Zak's face immediately changed. His lower lip jutted out. "My dad doesn't listen to me. Don't tell him you've seen me!"

"What will your family say when they find you're gone?" Leila looked worried.

"I'll think of something. I'm not a prisoner! I wanted to say hello!" Although Zak sounded defiant, Adam felt sorry for him. He was surely going to be in trouble.

"Come to the park! You *must* come to the park!" insisted Zak. "You can take turns on my skateboard."

Adam glanced at his watch. If they didn't set off for home right away, they would be later than the time Mama expected them. But how could they say no? Zak had come especially to see them.

Leila's eyes flashed to her brother, pleading. "We can be quick!"

"Come on, Adam!" coaxed Zak. "Ten minutes! Just don't tell anyone, hey!"

Although the park was in the opposite direction to the Northwest Gate, it wasn't far away. Zak steered his skateboard in front of them, keeping an eye out ahead for pedestrians as well as turning back to continue chatting. He asked about Mama and Grandma and other news from the neighborhood, including the yellow parakeet.

"Mama won't let us go that way anymore!" Leila blurted. "We can only go to the market with her, and she only uses the main streets."

"So, she's your guard now?"

"Her permit isn't renewed yet." Adam bridled at the

touch of mocking in the word *guard*.

"Okay, I see," replied Zak. He checked for cars before skating across the road to the other side. Adam and Leila followed.

A high stone wall surrounded the park. Someone had scrawled large graffiti, including hearts with letters for names. The paint wasn't there the last time he'd been there. He knew what their father would have said about beautiful old stone being defaced with paint. Zak suddenly sped up on his skateboard, leaping up toward the wall, skimming it, and then bouncing back onto the pavement. He swiveled around at the park entrance with a grin, waiting for his friends to catch up.

"Who wants this?" He held up his board.

"I'll go first!" stated Leila, handing her flute case to Adam. "It's only fair because Mama wouldn't let me come with you last time."

"Okay, fine." Adam was happy for his sister to take the skateboard. It was weeks ago that he and Zak had come to the park together, but clearly her memory of being excluded still stung.

He sat on a bench with their instrument cases, remembering that last time. Would he still be able to balance with both feet like he had managed in the end—or would he need to start all over again by just walking with the board? Now that he was preparing for the concert, he was even more nervous about falling and hurting his arm or hand.

In contrast, his sister seemed totally free from nerves, thriving on Zak's encouragement.

"Great, Leila! Do an ollie!"

"I've forgotten how!" She giggled.

"Come, I'll show you again!" Leila skidded to a stop and Zak jumped on to take her place. "Turn your front foot sideways. Sweep it up the deck like this!" Their laughter rang out across the park whenever she came off the skateboard. Adam hadn't heard her laugh like that for weeks.

For a while Adam enjoyed watching them, especially Zak's clowning. But when he checked the time again, he saw that twenty minutes had already passed. Adam hadn't yet had his turn and it would take at least forty minutes to get home. If they stayed any longer, Mama would be really frantic. He should have known they would never be quick in the park! If Little Jabari could speak, he would surely reproach him too. How could he have agreed to come with Zak immediately after Mr. B's praise for practicing so hard?

Adam signaled to Leila and Zak. "We have to go, Leila, right away!" He held out her flute case.

"It's your turn, Adam!" Zak protested. "Just five minutes?"

Adam shook his head. "I'll go first next time!" he said, and began walking with his violin case to the park entrance. Reluctantly, Leila followed.

"We'll see you again, Zak!" Adam called over his shoulder. He half expected him to stay behind in the park to practice more tricks. But a few seconds later, Zak overtook them on his skateboard, then slowed to their walking pace.

"Maybe! If my dad finds out where I've been, I don't know when you'll see me again!" Zak pouted, sweeping his finger across his throat. Although Zak said it like a joke, Adam knew he wouldn't like to be on the receiving end of Uncle Musa's anger.

They continued downhill together in friendly silence. Adam planned to take the small street ahead on the right. It would be shorter than carrying straight on down the hill with Zak. But at the corner of their turnoff, just as they were slapping hands to say goodbye, Adam spotted a group of teenage Permitted boys walking up the hill toward them. Zak turned and saw them. Adam felt a chill. One of them was the boy with the close-cut sandy hair and suspicious blue eyes whose father had forced Adam to open his violin case after evicting Aunt Hala from her house in the alley!

"It's him, isn't it?" Leila had recognized him too.

In a flash, Zak was speeding downhill on his skateboard toward them.

"No, Zak, no!" Adam wanted to yell, but the words froze. Zak was zooming toward the wall next to the group. This was madness! In a split second, he had bounced off the wall with his skateboard, skimming past the young men, who stumbled over each other as they jumped aside. Seconds later, they were brandishing fists, shouting at Zak as he disappeared around the next corner.

It looked as if the young Permitteds were shaken, but no one had been hurt. Had Zak just wanted to give them a big fright? But why didn't he stop to think? What if someone hadn't gotten out of the way in time? If there had been a crash, Zak could have been caught! For the moment, he may have gotten away, but he'd left his friends right there! Adam stood transfixed, feeling Leila close beside him, until one of the group stepped forward, pointing at them. It was the blue-eyed boy from the alley! Had he recognized them from their music cases?

The young Permitted began sprinting up the hill toward them, with one of his friends close behind. "Quick!" Adam pulled Leila into the side street, and they began to run. Another street forked off to the left but there were more shops and people on the road straight ahead. They chose the busier route. More cover, thought Adam. He pushed aside Dad's voice saying, *If you run, they'll say you're guilty.* This was one of those times you *had* to run.

"Pardon! Pardon!" they gasped, darting between pedestrians while trying not to knock anyone with their cases. All the people seemed to be Nons. If their chasers asked about two children with music cases, would anyone point them out?

"The bookshop, Adam!" Leila was panting. If they could get to Dad's favorite bookshop, they could hide there for a little. But it was still a few streets away.

"Stop those two!" A shrill voice sliced the air. "Stop

them!" Adam caught Leila's despairing glance just before a whirl of purple material enveloped them both and they were whisked through a doorway.

Seconds later, they were crouching behind a shop counter next to a woman in a tunic made of the same purple fabric. She was rapidly wrapping up the material, which was covered with small blue flowers, the same sky blue as her headscarf. Then she flung a length of shimmering silky orange over the counter, allowing one end to fall and drape over them.

The orange tent had just settled when rushing footsteps barged into the shop. The floorboards vibrated. "Have you seen two kids with music cases?" It was the same piercing voice, except now they could hear it was trembling with anger. Adam's heart was beating its timpani drums.

"This is a fabric shop. We make clothes. We don't get children here unless their mothers bring them for a fitting." The lady's tone was cool and precise. Leila bit on her thumb and Adam his lip. They held their breath, dreading that the orange material would be ripped away. Instead, the footsteps retreated as noisily as they had entered. There was no goodbye.

The woman in purple insisted they should come with her to a room at the back. Her assistant would look after the shop. Adam's timpani drums kept on rolling, although more quietly now as they sat in silence on a small floral settee next to a desk and watched the woman who had saved them bring three glasses of water on a tray. She pulled up a chair close and invited them to drink.

"You go to the music school, don't you? My nephew Sari takes lessons there, so I attend your concerts." She continued while they drank the water. "Now tell me, why were those boys chasing you?"

Adam hesitated. She was bound to ask their names. This was all going to get back to Mama, and as soon as the word *skateboard* entered the story, Mama would know Zak was involved . . . and then Uncle Musa would know.

"Our friend was skateboarding. He went too close, and some Permitted boys were frightened." Leila swished her right palm over her left. "But he never knocked into anyone!"

"They began chasing us, so we ran!" Adam's hands flew up as if to say, *What could we do?*

As Adam predicted, Sari's aunt wanted to know their names. On hearing their surname, she immediately said how sorry she was that they had lost their father, and what a loss his death was to all Nons. She would call their mother immediately to explain where they were.

"Please don't say anything about our friend with the skateboard!" The anxiety in Adam's voice made Sari's aunt raise her eyebrows.

"Well, I'll leave that to you. I just need to tell your

mother that you were being chased but you're safe now. It's nearly time to shut the shop so I'll drop you at home. You live inside the Stone City, don't you? It's not far."

Adam didn't ask how she knew. It must have to do with knowing about Dad.

Less than a couple of hours ago, their mother would have been so happy to hear Mr. B's praise of "Excellent progress!" But now everything had come smashing down to earth.

A DREADFUL SILENCE

"KEEP ZAK OUT OF THIS," Adam whispered to Leila as they waited for Sari's aunt to lock up the shop. At the same time, he was trying not to think of Zak's fate if the Permitteds caught him.

"How?" Leila mouthed back. "Mama will be certain to find out. It'll be worse if we lie!"

Adam knew she was right. Could they at least persuade Mama not to tell Uncle Musa? He would promise her that if Zak came again to music school, he would be firm about getting home to practice for the concert. Anyway, wasn't that the most important thing at the moment? It was essential to his plan. None of this would have happened if only he had told Zak that they couldn't go with him.

———

The children ran up the stone steps while Sari's aunt waited below in her small kingfisher-blue car. Mama hurried down to thank her. "Please come for coffee when you're free. You have my number now." It seemed to Adam that they exchanged more than smiles.

Later, what Adam would remember from that evening was Mama's worrying silence. At first Adam did the talking. He began with how Zak had been waiting with his skateboard outside music school and how he had been so happy to see them again. They had agreed to walk with him for a bit, as it wasn't far out of their usual way home. Skipping over their visit to the park, Adam told Mama about the young Permitteds coming up the hill and how they had recognized the boy from the family who evicted Aunt Hala. On the spur of the moment, Zak had sped ahead, shaving past the Permitted group with his skateboard trick on the wall beside them . . . and the next thing Adam and Leila knew, they were being chased.

"We didn't do anything, Mama!" Leila butted in. "No one got hurt! It was nothing like what happened to Aunt Hala!"

Adam was aware of Grandma coming from her bedroom to listen. Grandma was mostly quiet these days, but for Mama to say nothing was unusual. She didn't even ask about Zak.

"Please, Mama, please don't tell Uncle Musa!" Adam made his appeal. "Zak feels like a prisoner because he's not allowed to come home. He only wanted to see us. Leila's right. I know what he did was crazy. Maybe those boys got a fright. But that's all!"

Mama still said nothing. No further questions. No lecture—not at dinner and not after dinner. Just a terrible quiet.

When Adam retreated to his bedroom with his violin, Mama's silence followed like a shadow. He couldn't even focus on his scales. When he began playing Vivaldi's "Spring," instead of feeling that he and Little Jabari were flying through a valley, Zak kept flashing into his mind, speeding down the hill, bouncing the skateboard onto the wall, then disappearing around the corner. But did he get away? What if the Permitteds had caught him?

Adam gave up trying to practice. His mind was now whirling. If only they had left the park earlier. . . . If only he had grabbed Zak and pulled him into the side street. . . . If only he had told Zak they had to go straight home. . . . If only Dad were here to say something . . . help sort things out . . . If only Mama weren't so silent.

SILENCE

Mr. B says
silence has weight.
A violinist must feel it,
weigh it,
balance it
with sound.

But tonight
Mama's silence
is so heavy,
it weighs down everything.
No sound can balance
such dreadful silence.

NIGHT RAID

ADAM WOKE TO A THOUSAND drums and cymbals, banging and clashing on the other side of his door, swamping Mama's cries of "Wait! Wait!" Moments later, he was surrounded by shadowy bodies and flashlights. Even in the dark, he sensed rifles pointing at him. When the bedroom light was switched on, he froze at how close they were. His heart's timpani drums threatened to burst out.

"Get up! Hurry! Come, come, come!" A short, helmeted figure seized his school trousers from the rail at the end of his bed and slung them at him. Adam pulled them on mechanically. He could hear Mama's pleas in the next room.

"He's only twelve! A child! What has he done? Why do you want him?" She was repeating herself because no one was answering her. Two Permitted police were now rummaging through his closet and bookcase. A third officer guarded the door. With their domed black helmets, strapped around their cheeks and chins, they looked more alien than human.

"Who gave you this?" the Short One growled, his thumb flicking through the pages of Adam's book of folktales. It had been on top of Adam's bookcase, its cover of a flame-red horse stamping on the tail of the shrieking Firebird. "Huh?" The Short One jutted his chin toward Adam. "What's a boy like you doing with fairy tales?"

Adam's tongue felt completely dry . . . as dry as the time he had visited the desert with Dad. Now he was alone. But before he could think what to say, they were interrupted by the Tall One lobbing his violin case onto his bed.

"Open it!"

Adam's fingers stiffened as he released the catches. He wanted to yell "No!" and grab his precious violin to protect it from being handled by the helmeted invaders. But a glance at Little Jabari cautioned him—reminded him. *Use your head as well as your heart to stop an explosion.*

Adam pursed his lips as the Tall One grasped the violin and shook it. Did he expect something to fall out? When he found nothing, he let the violin dangle carelessly from his fingers. Adam lunged forward and just saved it from crashing to the floor. His hands shaking, he returned the violin to its case. A picture flashed into his head of Uncle Yosef carefully handing this same violin to young Grandma, trusting her to keep it safe and give it to Tomas. In Adam's mind, Uncle Yosef had kind eyes. Grandma had glimpsed tears in them . . . the very opposite of the harsh, ruthless eyes glaring beneath the Permitted helmets in his room.

The Short One had lost interest in Adam's bookcase and moved to his chest of drawers. Mama often complained that Adam should take more care putting away his clothes, but the Short One didn't care if he left a mess. What was he hoping to find in a drawer full of socks?

It was only when the Short One triumphantly clenched a small black cotton bag that Adam remembered the special present from Dad. Soon after turning twelve, he had been allowed to join weekend volunteers on an archaeological dig for Iron Age and Roman remains near an old Non village. Afterward, Dad had given him a set of small ancient stones as a memento. Adam gripped his arms around his chest to dampen the timpanis.

"So, you keep stones, huh? Good at throwing, are you?"

The Short One threw the little bag to the guard at his door. These police must be raiding the whole house! Had they come because the Permitted boy from the alley had recognized him and Leila? Were they still looking for Zak? Did they think *he* knew where Zak was? All he wanted to do was to get back under his blanket and pull it over his head . . . and end the nightmare.

Without warning, the Tall One jerked him forward, bringing Adam's nose up against his flak jacket. He felt the wrench in his shoulders as both arms were yanked behind him. His wrists were twisted and, with a quick sharp scraping sound, handcuffed. The rest was a daze as the Tall One and the Short One hauled him out of his bedroom, across the living room, and toward the front door. They barked at Mama to get out of the way as she tried to reach him, to touch him. He glimpsed Leila clutching Grandma, faces pale as ghosts. Then something was pulled across his eyes and all was darkness.

LEILA

NO TIME FOR SECRETS

GRANDMA'S GRIP ON HER HAND is so tight that it hurts. If anyone tries to pry her away, Leila knows Grandma will resist. The invasion in the middle of the night has stirred a sudden fierceness. Grandma's fury is strangely comforting and helps to calm Leila. She is terrified one of the invaders will look into her eyes. She buries her face in Grandma's gown, trying to forget the jumble of images in her head. . . . Adam pulling her . . . shouts of "Stop them!" . . . Zak skimming his skateboard against the wall above Permitted boys . . . Sari's aunt hauling them into her shop . . . trembling under orange cloth beside Adam, hearing, *Have you seen two kids with music cases?*

A commotion outside Adam's bedroom door makes Leila look up. Surrounded by armed police in enormous helmets and flak jackets, her brother has shrunk to a puppet. His dazed brown eyes are so wide they almost touch his bangs.

"Handcuffing a child! Shameless!" Grandma cries out. Mama stretches her arms to reach Adam but is slapped aside. A strip of black cloth is thrown over Adam's eyes and tied behind his head.

"Where are you taking him? Where? Just tell me where!" Mama demands and pleads. No answer. Seconds later, Adam is bundled out of the front door into the night.

Grandma and Leila sit huddled on either side of Mama on the settee. Mama rests her forehead on her knees. She clasps her hands over her head as she struggles against sobs. Grandma strokes her back while Leila slips her arm through Mama's, pulling herself as close as possible.

Gradually, Mama's breathing evens out. She sits up, swiveling toward Leila.

"Is there anything else you need to tell me before I ring Uncle Musa?"

Now it is Leila who is sobbing.

"I'm so—so—so sorry, Mama. If I hadn't played on Zak's skateboard in the park, we'd never have seen those Permitteds with that boy from the alley! We did nothing, I promise! They came up the hill just when we were saying goodbye. Adam and Zak slapped hands and . . ." Leila doesn't finish because Mama's palms rise like startled birds.

"Don't you see?" Mama whispers. "When those Permitted boys saw Adam and Zak slapping hands, what do you think they imagined? I can guess what they told the police. . . ." Mama's voice suddenly swells. "It was something bad, for sure."

She pushes herself upright off the settee to survey the room. Cupboard doors hang open. Pots, pans, lids, and the contents of the cutlery drawer are scattered over the kitchen counter. Books are strewn across the dining table and sitting room floor. Mama's red shoebox lies tipped on its side. The empty box stares up at them. Have the police taken her documents, or did they toss them among everything else?

Mama steps toward the table but then stops and turns to Leila.

"Bring me my phone."

By the time Uncle Musa arrives, only Grandma is still in her nightclothes. Mama is picking up pieces of paper from the floor and placing them back in the red box. She can't tell yet whether any are missing.

The shadows under Uncle Musa's eyes are darker than ever. Zak has gone missing again. Uncle Musa's brother says he didn't return from school, and the police raided both homes in the middle of the night. They want "the boy with the skateboard."

Uncle Musa can't hide his worry and anger. "Why did the police come for Adam?" His hands are shaking.

"Tell Uncle Musa, Leila. Tell him everything you know," says Mama, her voice low and insistent. "This is no time for secrets."

Uncle Musa sits opposite Leila at the kitchen table, Mama on one side and Grandma on the other. Leila feels tears rising again, but Grandma's hand is patting her knee and steadies her.

Leila recounts everything from the time Zak appeared outside music school, including her long turn on the skateboard in the park. She keeps her eyes fixed on the table until she comes to telling how Zak flew past the Permitteds.

"No one got hurt, Uncle Musa!" Leila makes herself look up. He *has* to see that she is telling the truth. "Believe me, no one!"

However, like Mama, he reacts badly when Leila describes how Zak and Adam slapped hands to say goodbye. He thumps his fists on the table, shaking his head.

"Do you think the police have got Zak too?" Leila asks Uncle Musa.

"We don't know where he is. But now that the police have Adam, they'll want him to tell them everything he knows."

Uncle Musa stops abruptly. He and Mama exchange one of those adult looks when there is something they would rather not say in front of a child.

Uncle Musa glances at his watch. The kitchen clock shows five a.m. "I'll call the lawyer at eight. He'll link us to someone who represents children in detention."

Children in detention! The words spark through Leila's head. Adam is "*in detention.*" Maybe Zak is too. Or will be . . . as soon as the police find him.

Mama gets up to make coffee, but Uncle Musa insists on going home. He'll try for an appointment as soon as possible and Leila will have to come with them.

"The lawyer must hear everything," says Uncle Musa, opening the door. It is still pitch-dark outside.

As the door closes, Leila throws her arms around Mama. "I'm scared," she whispers, clasping Mama's waist. "Adam must be *really* scared!"

Grandma, who has been very quiet, now lets out a massive sigh. ". . . and the poor boy doesn't have his violin to comfort him."

MS. ROTH

MAMA KEEPS LEILA HOME FROM school. "Go back to bed. I'll wake you if Uncle Musa gets an appointment." But Leila insists on staying close to Mama and Grandma, who are in the kitchen. She bundles up the duvet from her bed and covers herself on the settee but can't fall asleep.

In the end, Grandma rescues her. Will Leila help her make cookies?

"We'll keep some for Adam, won't we, Grandma?"

Grandma nods, kneading the dough.

"These are his favorites." Leila's eyes are becoming wet again as she stirs the chopped nuts into a bowl. She wants to ask how long the cookies will stay fresh in a tin but doesn't. Usually, Grandma's cookies are eaten within a day.

When the cookies go into the oven, Mama instructs

Leila to change from her jeans and T-shirt into a dress so she will be ready for the lawyer.

"Why can't I go like this, Mama?" However, one look at her mother's face tells Leila not to argue. She chooses her green print with small pink butterflies, then curls up on the settee with a book of poems. But the words are erased by memories of dark figures shunting a puppet across the living room. She lets everything blur.

Leila wakes with Mama's hand in hers. "Uncle Musa is here." It is midday and his brother is waiting with his taxi at the bottom of the steps. Zak's mother will stay with Grandma.

In the back of the car next to Mama, Leila remembers the last time in the same taxi, the night Zak's uncle Rami drove them to the hospital. Adam was with them the night Dad died, when the rain made it hard to see anything outside in the dark. Today is bright and sunny, but what's it like to be blindfolded?

Leila sees that they are now driving near her school . . . and Adam's. There's an empty desk in each of their classrooms. She and Adam are hardly ever out sick. Surely no one will imagine that Adam has been *blindfolded* and taken to *prison*?

The car pulls up outside tall green metal gates. Uncle Musa, Mama, and Leila clamber out.

"Call me when you're ready," says Uncle Rami. "I won't be far."

A man lets them in and the gate clangs behind them. Leila holds Mama's hand tightly as they ascend the wide steps of a large building with stones the same color as music school. They follow Uncle Musa to the front desk, where the receptionist recognizes him. She gives Leila a special smile, but Leila's lips are pressed tight. The receptionist nods sympathetically and rings for Uncle Musa's friend.

They sit in the waiting area. There are signs on the wall with the names of organizations and people who rent offices in the building. Leila is reading the signs when a group of young people walk down the stairs chatting and laughing. They look like students.

"Applying for scholarships, I expect," Mama says quietly as their voices fade outside. The word *scholarship* startles Leila. They haven't yet heard whether they can have scholarships toward their school fees next year, including music school. Uncle Elias, who is paying their fees, helped Mama write the letters. But what will happen now that the police have taken Adam? Leila's shoes begin mechanically tapping on the wooden floor until Mama's eyes flash at her.

The silence breaks when Uncle Musa's friend arrives. He is the lawyer who is trying to obtain Mama's permission to stay. His mustache needs a trim and he has shadows under his eyes, but he smiles when Mama introduces Leila. She thinks his face looks kind but, once again, her lips won't move.

"You're in the best hands with my colleague Lily Roth for this," the lawyer says, leading them down a corridor. "Sadly, we have too many of these cases, and our other colleague who represents children is in court today." He stops outside a door. "You've probably seen Lily Roth on television. There aren't many Permitted lawyers who speak out like she does." His voice drops. "She can be quite a dragon. You'll see!" He knocks on the door and ushers them in.

A short woman with a bob of unruly gray hair and glasses rises from her desk beside a huge bookcase. She shakes all their hands but when she comes to Leila, the lawyer holds on to her hand for a couple of moments.

"So, this is about your brother . . . and his friend?" She speaks to them in Non but with a strong Permitted accent. The searching brown eyes behind the glasses remind Leila of her school principal. They are eyes that say *I want the truth and nothing but the truth*.

"The police took her brother away early this morning!" Mama's voice is close to breaking.

"And my son . . . he's missing—" Uncle Musa breathes heavily.

Ms. Roth pulls three chairs nearer her desk. "Please sit down," she says. "We need to start at the beginning."

"Let me know when you've finished," Uncle Musa's

friend murmurs. He shuts the door behind them with barely a sound.

Later, Leila will think that Ms. Roth is a mixture of an archaeologist, a detective, and a filmmaker. She begins by digging up what has happened, searching for any missing pieces. It seems that she is running everything through her head like a film, before tapping on her keyboard. She asks Leila to take her through exactly what happened, scene by scene, after Zak met her and Adam outside music school. She wants every detail. When it comes to how Zak and Adam said goodbye, she stretches a hand across her desk and asks Leila to demonstrate.

At the end of Leila's account, Ms. Roth takes her back again to the beginning. This time Leila remembers the graffiti on the park wall and how Zak had sped up on his skateboard, flying up at the wall, then bouncing back onto the pavement. Ms. Roth leans forward. Leila feels the truth-seeker eyes on her, sharp as lasers.

"Is that something that Zak likes to do on his skateboard?"

"It's one of his best tricks!"

"I see . . ." Ms. Roth's fingers move quicker than ever on the keyboard. A little later, she returns to Zak's tricks. This time, Leila recalls how he loved to demonstrate his skills when they walked through the Stone City.

"So, could Zak have been showing off a bit yesterday?" Ms. Roth rests back in her chair, thoughtful. "I mean, when he leaped with his skateboard against the wall near those Permitted boys?"

Leila nods, although she doesn't want to say anything bad about Zak. Ms. Roth raises her eyebrows.

"Ah! That's very helpful; thank you, Leila."

They wait for the lawyer to explain.

"There's a lot we can't be certain about at the moment, but I suspect those Permitted boys have lodged a complaint with the police. They may have said: *A Non boy on a skateboard attacked us. He would have injured us if we didn't jump out of the way.* They may even have said, *He had a weapon, a knife.*"

"That's not true!" Leila cries. Mama's hand clasps her mouth and Uncle Musa breathes even more heavily than before. It seems that Ms. Roth has just confirmed Mama's and Uncle Musa's worst fears.

"I believe you, Leila." Ms. Roth's voice softens. "Thank you for telling me everything so clearly." She reaches for her telephone. "Now I must find where the police have taken Adam . . . and whether they have Zak."

On the phone, Ms. Roth speaks in Permitted. Most of the time, Leila can't follow what she's saying. Instead, she watches Ms. Roth raise her eyebrows, shake her head, and throw up her free hand every now and again. Then her voice sharpens and there's fire in her eyes. She lashes out words. The person at the other end of the phone is stalling and blocking her. What did Uncle Musa's friend say? *She can be quite a dragon.* Leila's stomach lurches. Even with the dragon-lady lawyer on their side, it will be a struggle to get her brother back.

Suddenly she hears Zak's name. The response is short, and Ms. Roth puts down the phone. She explains. The officer in charge at the central police station refuses to comment on Zak and won't say where Adam is being held.

"This is the usual," Ms. Roth adds grimly. "They don't like giving information until absolutely necessary. Sometimes they take a child to a local police station, but they usually end up at the central station for questioning."

"Please! Tell those police that my son only loves his violin! He lives for his music; that's the truth!" Mama's voice trembles. "Tell them . . . ," she says, struggling to steady her speech, "that he carries a bow in his violin case, not a knife!"

"I understand." Ms. Roth rises from her chair. "I promise that I'll do my very best for Adam and Zak. I'll call you as soon as I have news." She walks around her desk to shake all their hands again.

"You know, I have a granddaughter the same age as you, Leila." Ms. Roth is still holding her hand. Leila looks up and their eyes meet. "You are being very brave. But . . . it *shouldn't* be this way. No." Ms. Roth's gray bob of hair shakes with the force of her words. At the same time, her hand feels surprisingly gentle before she lets go of Leila's.

"Do you have a picture of her—your granddaughter?" Leila surprises herself with her sudden boldness. She had glimpsed a photo inside a silver frame on Ms. Roth's desk. The lawyer stretches out for the frame and passes it to Leila.

"This is Rachel."

A girl with long dark hair in two high ponytails, in the same style that Leila likes, stares directly up at her. Her smile and eyes look slightly cheeky.

"Come, Leila. Ms. Roth has work to do." Mama's voice brings her back to the room.

"It's fine," says Ms. Roth, but Leila is already handing back the photo in its frame. If she has any further questions, this is not the time.

Uncle Musa's lawyer friend greets them in the corridor. As they follow him out of the building, he speaks in a low voice to the adults.

"I'm still waiting to hear from the Department of the Interior."

"Thank you." Mama's voice is also muted but Leila hears. "I hope this trouble with my son won't affect the outcome."

Raising both hands to chest height, he softly pats the air in front of him. "Let's take it one step at a time."

NEWS SPREADS

UNCLE MUSA'S BROTHER IS WAITING outside. Inside the car, Mama leans forward. Will he drive them past the central police station on the way home? A few minutes later, they slow down. On the right are high stone walls, topped with barbed wire. Above, the sky is clear blue. Outside the walls, they are free to look up . . . but if Adam is inside, what can he see? Is he still blindfolded? Aren't prisons very dark, like dungeons?

Leila grips Mama's hand. As Uncle Rami drives on, Leila studies the route. She hopes she can remember it. If Adam is behind those walls, at least she wants to know the way.

Leila automatically puts a plate out for Adam as she lays the table. As soon as she realizes what she has done, she pulls the plate away with a fierce shake of her head.

The telephone rings just as they are about to have supper. It's Ms. Roth.

"So, Adam is at the central station . . . and they've *already* taken him to court?" Mama repeats to be doubly sure. Leila and Grandma wait until Mama puts down the phone to hear what has happened. Ms. Roth is angry because it seems that a judge has given the police another twenty-four hours to question Adam. If they want to keep him longer, they must bring him back to court again. Ms. Roth has also told the police to notify her before they interrogate Adam. He is a child and either she or Mama must be allowed to be present when he is questioned.

"And Zak, Mama?" Leila bites her thumb.

"They still won't say anything. Ms. Roth says she'll call Uncle Musa now."

"Oh, how that family is suffering. . . ." Grandma shakes her head. "Not even to know where the boy is. . . ."

Leila wants to say that although they might know where Adam is, it's horrible not knowing what the police are doing to him. But she doesn't. Grandma and Mama must know more than she does about what can happen to a Non child in a Permitted prison.

In the morning, Leila begs not to go to school. "Please, Mama, let me stay! If they take Adam to court today, I want to go with you! I want to see him, please!"

Mama is adamant. "You have to go to school, Leila. You

missed so much already." Leila knows she's referring to when Dad died. "I'll collect you on the way if I hear anything."

"But what if those Permitted boys see me going to school? The one in Aunt Hala's house will recognize me!"

"You're not walking to school by yourself," declares Mama. "I'm coming with you."

"Then Grandma will be all alone!" exclaims Leila.

"I'll be all right," insists Grandma. "It's best that your mother takes you."

"But if that boy is with his father, they'll do something to *both* of us!"

"Oh, Leila . . . Leila!" Mama's and Grandma's voices overlap.

"Don't frighten yourself," says Mama. "We'll get through this." Then, as if everything is normal, Mama reminds Leila to take her flute. It's a music school day.

Leila feels everyone's eyes on her and Mama as they arrive at the school gate. Has news about Adam spread already?

Inside the office, the principal's forehead knits with concern as she listens to Mama. Afterward, she turns to Leila.

"I know it will be hard to focus on your schoolwork. If you feel overwhelmed at any time, come to my office. You can talk or just sit quietly here with a book."

Leila struggles to say, "Thank you."

After Mama hugs her goodbye, panic strikes. She wants to run after Mama. But an arm around her shoulder restrains her and leads her to class.

In math class, Leila lets her head fill with numbers. The next lesson is English, normally her favorite. Today, they have to answer questions on a passage in their textbook. It's about a boy called Oliver, who is badly treated and starving. Yet when he begs for food and says, "Please, sir, I want some more," he is locked in a "dark and solitary room."

Leila's mind flies to Adam. Is her brother alone? Is he hungry? Is he somewhere dark? How can people treat children like this! Her eyes feel hot and damp, but she doesn't want to cry in front of everyone. She clenches her fists under the desk. Their teacher is explaining that the story is set long ago. The author didn't say that people in the story were Permitteds and Nons, but, if you were poor, you were treated very badly. One of the worst places was the "workhouse." Oliver was born in one.

"That's slavery! Did the poor people protest?"

"Do they still have workhouses?"

"They treated poor children like they were nothing!"

Leila remains quiet, but the indignation in voices around her is comforting. The class quiets to write answers to the questions beneath the passage. When the bell rings, they put their books away and stand in silence behind their desks. Waiting to be dismissed, Leila hears her name. The teacher addresses her, in front of everyone.

"Leila, you should know that we all hope your brother and his friend will come home safely . . . and soon."

All eyes are on her again. This time, she feels a little less alone.

THE FLUTE'S MESSAGE

THE CLASS IS SETTLING DOWN after morning break when the principal comes to the door and signals Leila to come. She grabs her schoolbag and flute case. Mama should have let her stay at home! Yet she has kept her promise. Adam is being taken to court any time now. Zak's uncle is outside school with his car engine running. Leila scrambles after Mama into the back seat.

Mama keeps checking her phone for a message from Ms. Roth with the number of the courtroom. Ms. Roth has already warned Mama that the police will move Adam very quickly in and out of the building and that the hearing won't last long. They won't be allowed to talk with Adam but at least they'll see him. The police will probably ask the judge for more time to question him. Ms. Roth will argue that the police have no case, but the judge is more likely to listen to the police.

Uncle Rami stops the car opposite a long gray building with metal barriers in front of the main door. People are milling around on the pavement. Most look like Nons. Leila and Mama squeeze their way toward the doorway. With her schoolbag bumping on her back and her flute case strapped over shoulder, Leila tries not to knock anyone. However, the doorway is blocked. A man and a woman in blue uniforms are checking bags. They must wait for their turn.

Mama's phone pings. Ms. Roth has sent the court number, which means that the police are already inside the building and on their way to the courtroom with Adam. The hearing could be over before they get there! If Adam looks for them, he will think they haven't come. Leila's heart is pounding. Mama sends a text to Ms. Roth. Leila stares at the two bag checkers with their bored faces, willing them to go faster . . . *please, faster*!

Finally, it's their turn. Leila must open her schoolbag and flute case.

"What's all this?" The woman sweeps her hand over the three sections of Leila's flute, neatly packed in the case.

"It's a flute. She has a lesson this afternoon," Mama replies for Leila. Her voice is terse.

"Take them out. Let me look inside."

Leila's face feels hot. What does this Permitted think she has hidden? Mama's hand gently squeezes her shoulder. It's Mama's signal to stay calm! Leila carefully picks up her flute's head joint. The officer takes it from her and makes a show of checking inside the metal tubing. Leila keeps a straight face until the woman probes the mouthpiece with her forefinger. Leila's top lip curls up in disgust even though Mama's hand is pressing more deeply. When the officer points to the next piece in the case, Leila straightens her face but makes a show of carefully placing her fingers around the buttons on the main body of her flute so as not to damage them. But the officer grasps the main section carelessly, then peers down the central hole at each end. Leila knows that she's looking for a reason to confiscate it. A picture jumps into her mind of the Permitted man forcing Adam to open his violin case outside Aunt Hala's house. *What's a Non boy like you doing with a beautiful violin like this?* This Permitted woman also doesn't think that a Non girl can own a musical instrument! Leila knows she mustn't do anything rash, but while the officer takes her time examining the foot joint, Leila smoothly assembles the head and body of her flute. As soon as the officer has finished with the foot section, Leila picks it up and twists it on too.

"There!" she declares. She knows she mustn't sound defiant. "You can see it's only my flute."

With a flick of her hand, the officer waves them away. Leila scurries to keep up with Mama down a corridor clustered with people, her case in one hand and her flute in the other. A door opens to their right and Leila glimpses a tall dark-eyed boy in handcuffs surrounded by police officers. It's not Adam, nor Zak. Two doors down, Mama halts, puts a finger to her lips, and pushes the door. Leila doesn't need a reminder to be quiet as the court usher leads them to seats at the back.

It takes Leila a few seconds to see Adam. He is sitting alone in a wooden box to one side of a raised desk. Leila thinks the man on top must be the judge. Ms. Roth is standing near Adam with her back to them. She is speaking to the judge in Permitted. Adam's head is bent down, his hair half covering his eyes, which seem fixed on Ms. Roth. How much can he understand of what the lawyer is saying? Even though they learn Permitted in school, Leila can only pick out the odd word like *child* and *school.* If only Adam would turn his head, he would know they were there.

Ms. Roth sits down and a man on the other side stands up. He wears a black cloak like Ms. Roth. There are police officers behind him, and Leila decides that he is on the side of the police. He doesn't speak for long but is brisk and confident. The judge announces his decision.

"One week!" Mama breathes heavily. "They will keep him for a whole week?" She rushes forward to reach Adam but already he is surrounded by police officers. Leila can't see her brother anymore—and he hasn't even seen them! The cluster of uniforms is moving toward the door. In a flash, she remembers her flute and lifts it to her lips.

The melody of "Ode to Joy" sails over the courtroom. For a moment, everything falls silent except for the notes rising from the flute. From the corner of her eyes, Leila can see that the police have stalled. Everyone is staring at her. She mustn't stop!

"Mama! Leila!" It's a desperate cry.

Is that Adam trying to peek between the steel-like arms? The police advance to the door while the court usher strides toward her. Leila lowers her flute. The usher wants to wrench it away. Luckily, Mama and Ms. Roth arrive beside her at the same time.

Ms. Roth addresses the usher. Although Leila can't follow everything, she hears the name "Beethoven." Ms. Roth sweeps up her hands, continuing to speak. Leila recognizes the Permitted word for *beautiful*. The lawyer is doing her best to calm the usher.

The conversation ends with a warning that Ms. Roth has to translate. The usher says that if Leila tries to play her flute again in here, she will be banned from the court. Leila is shaking inside but her mind is also leaping. Her flute told Adam that they were there!

Ms. Roth promises Mama that she will press for Adam's

release. “I don’t think they’ve found Zak yet,” she says bluntly. “That’s why they’re holding on to Adam . . . and without Zak, there’s no case.”

“That’s so unfair!” Leila can’t stop herself. “They just believe those Permitted boys! With my own eyes, I saw that Zak didn’t even touch them! He must be really scared and that’s why he’s hiding!” Mama pulls her close and Ms. Roth nods in sympathy.

“I’ll do my best,” she says.

It’s still an hour until her flute class and Leila is hungry, so Mama takes her to the café at the bookshop near music school. Dad’s friend Uncle Mikhail is delighted to see them. He sits them down with cake, coffee, and a chocolate milkshake for Leila. But his face clouds over when he hears about Adam.

“Outrageous! Adam is such a gentle boy!” His fingers press down on the table like roots steadying a tree. “I’ve seen his friend Zak on his skateboard. He’s lively . . . but to say he had a knife . . . and that Adam gave it to him! What a *disgraceful* lie!”

Leila usually savors every sip of her milkshake. But today her mind can only focus on the adult talk about the police raid and Grandma.

“Terrifying,” Uncle Mikhail mutters. “It must have brought back memories for Adam’s grandmother of when the police came for her son.”

It hadn't occurred to Leila. Grandma hadn't said it . . . but of course! She can't have forgotten the time Permitted police had raided her home and snatched away Dad when he was still a young man. First it was her son . . . and now her grandson.

Mama also tells Uncle Mikhail about Leila's message by flute inside the court. His face lights up. "Well done, young lady! Quick thinking! Your father would have cheered you." Leila is too choked up to respond.

Uncle Mikhail taps the fingers of one hand on the table. "I have a journalist friend who can perhaps help . . . by shining a light on this case."

"Thank you, Mikhail," says Mama. "But let me talk first with Zak's father and our lawyer. I'll let you know."

Leila is puzzled why Mama doesn't just say yes. Didn't Dad always speak about the importance of "shining a light"?

As soon as they leave the bookshop for music school, she asks, "Why didn't you want Uncle Mikhail to call his friend right away, Mama?"

Mama leads the way across the busy road without an answer. But when they enter the music school courtyard, she stops in the shade of a eucalyptus tree. They are early and the courtyard is still empty. Mama tilts her head and looks solemnly at Leila.

"I think Uncle Musa will agree about talking to this journalist, but we have to decide this together. It will suit the Permitted police if something divides our families."

Leila isn't sure that she understands about the families being divided, but right now she needs Mama to come inside the building and explain about Adam. Although everyone at music school surely knows about young Nons being arrested and thrown into prison, no one will have imagined it happening to Adam.

ZAK RETURNS

"DON'T FALL ASLEEP YET!" MAMA chides Leila at the back of the car. Her eyes are closing as Uncle Rami drives them home after her flute lesson. He doesn't mention Zak, although Leila is sure he must be thinking of him, just like they are thinking of Adam.

Uncle Rami leaves them at the stone steps leading up to their house.

"Thank you for your kindness," says Mama.

"Anytime! Our families are one." Uncle Rami waves as he drives away.

When Mama opens the front door, she gasps. Leila peers past her. Sitting at the table, with his head bent over a bowl, is Zak.

Grandma sits opposite, watching him wolf down bread and soup. Zak lifts his face toward the door. The usual liveliness in his eyes has vanished. In its place, there's misery. Without a word, he hunches back over the food.

"The poor boy hasn't eaten for two days," says Grandma, levering herself off her chair. "Come, let's all eat. I made a good bean soup."

"Thank you, Mother, that's most welcome." Mama's voice sounds deliberately calm.

Leila's head is buzzing. There is so much she wants to ask Zak . . . and tell him. So many crazy things have happened in just three days. Yet Grandma and Mama still try to go on as normal. A voice inside Leila suddenly wants to scream. Instead, she takes a deep breath.

"Help yourself," says Grandma, offering the fruit bowl to Zak. Without raising his eyes, he coils his fingers around a peach. Although he still hasn't said anything, Leila knows that he's listening when they describe for Grandma what happened in court. Even when Mama announces that Zak's father is on his way, he remains silent.

Uncle Musa arrives soon afterward, his face looking ready to explode. However, when Zak runs and throws himself into his father's arms, Uncle Musa wraps his arms around him. As they sway silently together, Leila wipes her eyes with the back of her hand. She glances at Grandma and Mama. Their eyes are wet too.

Uncle Musa coaxes Zak to tell his story.

"I'm sorry, Baba! When I saw that boy smiling with his friends—the one from the family that stole Aunt Hala's house—I felt so upset! Believe me, Baba, I only did my trick against the wall next to them. I didn't hurt anyone, Baba! I didn't touch anyone! But then they began chasing me, calling me 'Murderer!'"

Zak describes his escape and how he abandoned his skateboard, pushing it under a crate of lemons in front of a grocery shop. From there, he slipped into a crowd of tourists on their way into the Stone City. He stayed tucked in the middle, until they visited some ruins where he spotted a cave sunk below ground level. Sneaking away from the group, he hid behind a wall until evening, when the gates to the ruins were closed. As soon as he was alone, he climbed down to hide inside the cave. His only food had been a half-eaten sandwich left by a tourist.

"Why didn't you come home?" Uncle Musa's voice trembles.

"I was scared, Baba. That Permitted boy recognized me. One of them called me a murderer, Baba! I knew he'd tell the police that I attacked them!"

Uncle Musa sighs. There's a long pause. Everyone waits. At last, he resumes.

"Do you know about Adam? This 'trick' of yours brought the police to *this* house in the middle of the night to get him!"

Zak looks wretched but remains silent as his father continues. The police had also raided their home and that of Zak's cousins. In both places they left their threats. If

Uncle Musa doesn't bring Zak to them, the whole family will pay the price.

A picture from television news flashes into Leila's head, of a girl, her own age, watching a bulldozer break down the walls of her family's home—the living room, kitchen, bedrooms, everything. A Permitted soldier claimed that the girl's older brother had attacked one of their officers. His family had to be punished. Could that happen to Uncle Musa's home? Could it happen to Grandma's . . . theirs?

"So, what are you going to do, Musa?" Mama asks the question they all dread.

Leila has never seen Uncle Musa look so haggard. He closes his eyes, shaking his head. The air in the room is heavy until Zak breaks the silence. His voice is a hoarse whisper.

"Baba, let me come home tonight," he pleads. "One night, please! Tomorrow morning I'll go with you to the police station."

Uncle Musa's shoulders rise, then fall.

"We'll take the risk," he says softly. "Your mother and grandmother have cried so much . . . they won't forgive me if they can't have you under the same roof for these few hours."

A few minutes later, Mama, Grandma, and Leila cluster at the door, watching father and son descend the stone steps into the dark.

Leila can't sleep. She keeps thinking of Adam surrounded by Permitted police in the court. The image alternates with the usher's angry face looming down on her. Grandma breathes unevenly in her bed, as if she too is troubled by a nightmare, but she doesn't wake. In the end, Leila creeps out to make her way to Mama's bedroom. Her mother appears to be asleep, but as soon as Leila slips under the duvet cover, she feels an arm stretch out for her. With Mama's fingers resting lightly on her shoulder, Leila falls at last into deep sleep.

ADAM

THE MINOTAUR

THREE DESKS AND A LARGE filing cabinet filled the interrogation room at the central police station, leaving only a small space in the middle. Adam counted three Permitteds. The nearest to him did all the yelling. At first, he ordered Adam to stand on a spot in silence. The three men sat at their desks, sometimes chatting with one another but ignoring him from behind computers. After a while, Adam felt his legs wobble. When he asked to sit down, the nearest Permitted jumped up. His neck and head were as thick as the Minotaur's in his book of legends.

"Who do you think you are?" he bellowed. He jabbed an arm, like a horn, at Adam. "Wait until I speak to you!"

A little later, when pains began shooting up his legs, Adam tried shifting his weight from one foot to the other.

When he swayed, the Minotaur shouted, "Stand still! No moving!"

Eventually he allowed Adam to sit, but the chair was right next to the Minotaur's desk. There was no escape from the yelling.

"Why did you keep the knife for your friend?"

"You helped him, didn't you? That makes you GUILTY—just like your friend!"

It felt like his head was being bashed against a wall with cymbals crashing around him.

"Why do you cover for him? HE's not so loyal to YOU!"

As soon as Adam raised his hands to cover his ears, the Minotaur pulled them away.

"If you don't cooperate, your family will suffer! Is that what you want? IS THAT WHAT YOU WANT?"

"No! No!"

Adam's voice was smothered by a roar. "We know EVERYTHING ABOUT YOU! Your mother is waiting for a new permit, isn't she? So, you'd better tell us what really happened!"

Suddenly, the Minotaur sat down and one of the other men brought his chair closer. This man spoke quietly. He said he could help with the permit—but first Adam had to help them. Just tell them what had really happened. It would be best for Adam to talk sooner rather than later.

It was a relief not to have the screaming in his ears. Adam began, barely louder than a whisper, with how Zak had met him and Leila outside music school. How they had all gone to the park to play with Zak's skateboard. How they had been relaxing and enjoying themselves until they set off home. As he spoke, the Minotaur's fingers tapped heavily on his keyboard.

Adam stopped to swallow. He needed some water, but his interrogators were waiting for what happened next. So he explained how he and Zak had slapped hands to say goodbye and then Zak had skated off, leaping up against the wall near a group of Permitted boys who were coming up the hill. It was his best trick. There had been no knife, and no one was hurt. He had never known Zak to hurt anyone with his skateboard.

All the while, the Minotaur was typing. Adam continued. He and his sister had run away when they saw they were being chased. They had done nothing wrong but were scared. They didn't know what had happened to Zak. It was a shock when police came for Adam in the middle of the night.

Shortly after he finished speaking, a printer began buzzing and clicking. When the Minotaur stood up, he thrust a sheet of paper toward Adam.

"This is your statement. Sign it!"

Dad's voice shot into his head. *Never sign anything that you haven't read.*

"I'm thirsty. I need water."

"Not until you've signed your statement."

Adam glanced at the paper. The writing was in Permitted. He was learning the language in school, but he wasn't fluent. A lot of students didn't want to learn it at all. Adam stalled.

"I need time to read it."

"Then hurry up!" The Minotaur snorted. "You've wasted enough of our time already."

Letters and words jumped around on the page in front of him. It was only after the Minotaur left the room to make himself coffee that Adam took a deep breath and focused enough to see what he could recognize.

Halfway down, the word for *knife* caught his eye. Last week's Permitted spelling list included words for kitchen items. This had been one of them. But why was the word here? He had said clearly that there had been no knife. He searched the surrounding words for *no* or *not*. Neither was there.

Slowly Adam pieced together the sentence: "I gave the knife to my friend." He hadn't said that! His stomach churned. He had heard about young Nons who signed confessions in Permitted when they didn't know the language. If he signed this, Mama would get her permit. If he didn't, she wouldn't.

Sorry if you do. Sorry if you don't . . .

But this wasn't an old folktale. There was no horse of power to advise him. He covered his head with his hands.

Adam was still hunched over the chair when the Minotaur returned. A clenched fist thumped the table. "Have you signed?"

Adam shook his head. "I can't think. I can't think." He heard himself whimpering.

"If you don't sign this by TOMORROW, you'll know the real meaning of TROUBLE." The Minotaur signaled to a policewoman at the door to take Adam away.

His legs felt weak. He had to stop himself from leaning on the policewoman as she handcuffed him. Did they really think he could run away when he could barely stand? As they entered the corridor, a shrieking sound emerged from a couple of doors away. So raw and wild, it seemed hardly human. The policewoman marched Adam in the opposite direction, but the high-pitched cries followed him down the corridor. His heart pounded. Could it be Zak?

"THAT MAKES YOU GUILTY . . . !"

WHY DID YOU KEEP THE knife for your friend?

You helped him, didn't you? That makes you GUILTY . . . !

Why do you cover for him? HE's not so loyal to YOU!

It was the middle of the night and Adam couldn't sleep. The voice of his interrogator pierced his head while cold air rose from the concrete floor, attacking him through a thin, dirty blanket. Curled up, tight as an ammonite, on the narrow iron bed, Adam couldn't get rid of the accusations screamed at him a few hours earlier. He was desperate to sleep. The voice was stopping him. He had to chase it away . . . but how? It was somewhere deep inside him.

Stretching out his left arm from under the blanket, he forced himself to ignore the cold pricking his skin. Instead, he tried to imagine his palm and fingers ready to cradle Little Jabari. Now he raised his right arm to lift his bow.

One . . . two . . . three . . . four . . . Eyes closed, slowing his breath, he struggled to revive the melody that could take him flying bareback over the ancient hills, like Grandfather Tomas in the Time Before . . .

You kept the knife for your friend!

The harsh, insistent voice had returned, this time even more fortissimo. It was followed by fearful shrieks echoing down the Minotaur's corridor, filling his head and his cell. His music needed to be louder, more rousing. He should try "Ode to Joy" . . . slowing his breath once again . . . lifting his bow . . . the whole youth orchestra behind him . . . the choir raising their voices . . . Mr. B signaling, "Lift the roof!"

Knife . . . helped . . . GUILTY . . . Why do you cover for him?

And, finally, words that slithered deeper into him. . . .

HE's not so loyal to YOU!

Had they really caught Zak or were they pretending? Zak would never have said that Adam kept a knife for him. It wasn't true. There was no knife. Hadn't Dad always said that evidence has to be respected? *The artifacts we dig out of the earth don't lie, Adam. It's people who do that.* Dad's voice now sounded close enough to be in the same cell. How could he, Adam, sign the Minotaur's statement with its lies? But if he didn't, Mama wouldn't get her permit!

What would Dad do, faced with this choice? Hot tears coursed down Adam's cheeks.

He knew it was morning because of the square of light coming through the small window high above him. Adam perched on the corner of the iron bed, waiting for the clang of a key in the door. Although there was another bed along the opposite wall, he was alone in the small cell. At any moment, someone would come with handcuffs to take him to the interrogation room. It might even be the Minotaur. He pressed his thumb and fingers against his heart, trying to mute its thrumming. Instead, the vibration seemed to spread around his body. He had to take his mind away, out of this place.

Adam began humming his scales. At the same time, he moved the fingers of his left hand up and down the imaginary strings of Grandfather's violin, while Little Jabari kept his eyes on him. Starting with C major, he made his way through all the major keys, then the minors. Mr. B would make him repeat if not perfect. Adam kept humming and, for a short while, nothing else mattered.

Still, no one came for him. Part of his brain knew they were playing with him so that the Minotaur's threat and the shrieks down the corridor could do their work. Yet his scales had been calming and, suddenly, he knew the answer to his question, "What would Dad do?" Closing his eyes, he could hear his father's voice clearly. . . . *Stick to the truth, son.* Whatever their threats about Mama, he had to stick to the truth. Deep down Adam knew she would agree with that. She had already gotten him a lawyer. The woman with compelling eyes and wild gray hair was a Permitted, but she spoke kindly to him in the court. If he gave in to the lie about a knife, how could he ever return to the truth?

Adam threw himself on the bed, turning his face away from the door. He mustn't let himself think what the Minotaur would do. The Minotaur wanted him to tell lies about Zak. That was wrong. Wrong! Once again, he began humming his scales.

The clatter of metal jolted him, followed by a thud. The door clanked shut as Adam rolled over to see a figure crumpled on the concrete floor.

"Zak?" he whispered. "Zak!"

There was no response except for sobs.

"What have they done to you?" Adam crouched down on the cold floor beside his friend. Zak still wouldn't turn to show his face, even when Adam placed his hand gently on the back of his neck.

Adam knelt there for a while, his hand lightly patting Zak's shoulder. "I had to stand until my legs were too weak!" Adam whispered. "Did they do that to you too?" Zak's head moved a fraction. Whatever they had done to him must have been worse.

"Come, let me help you." Adam slipped a hand under Zak's arm. "It's better on the bed." Zak didn't resist. But when Adam tried to ease him off the floor, he stumbled under the weight. Zak had no energy in his legs, yet with great effort, he lifted his face. It was his eyes that shocked Adam the most. There had always been a spark in Zak's eyes, whatever his mood. Today, they were flat, almost dead.

Adam sat cross-legged, remaining close to his friend on the floor. Questions flooded in. Why had they put Zak in his cell? Was it a warning? If he refused to sign the Minotaur's statement, was this how he would end up? Or were there secret devices in the walls or ceiling, to listen to what he and Zak might say to each other? Wasn't that what Dad said about prison? You always knew someone could be watching or listening.

Adam felt a movement. Zak's ribs were juddering. He was shaking, crying. Once again, Adam rested his hand on Zak's shoulder, gently patting and stroking. It's what Grandma did when they were upset. He had never had to do that for anyone before. Gradually, Zak's sobs lessened. He was trying to say something, but the rhythm was jagged.

"Did—they—make—you sign?"

"They want me to," Adam muttered. "And you? Did you . . . ?"

A huge sob wracked through Zak. He clutched his arms around his chest, but it was like trying to stop a giant wave. Later, when his breathing calmed, with Adam's help, he managed to push himself up off the floor and sit on the edge of the bed. Adam sat next to him. For a while neither spoke until Zak began to whisper. Even whispering was an effort.

Zak had been threatened with twenty years in jail for trying to kill a Permitted if he didn't sign. If he pleaded guilty, it would be less. They had blindfolded him and made him sit on a low stool with his wrists tied together behind him. His back felt like it was going to break. He had begged to see his parents, but they said only if he signed. In the end, it was too much. He took their pen and signed their paper. He couldn't read Permitted but had guessed what it said.

All the time Zak spoke, he stared at his knees. Adam didn't know what to say. When Zak finally broke the silence, mumbling "I'm sorry," he still wouldn't look at Adam. Instead, he rolled over on the mattress with his back to him, shaking again, but this time making a low moaning sound. Adam returned to the opposite bed. He lay down and stared at the gray concrete ceiling.

The Minotaur would come for him anytime now. He was sure they had thrown Zak into his cell as a warning. Even after Zak fell asleep, his moans and whimpers remained in Adam's head. They formed a chorus behind a new voice that arrived from nowhere. *What's the point?* it asked dully, over and over. Adam had no answer.

Zak had signed a statement saying that he had tried to kill a Permitted. So, what would he, Adam, achieve by refusing to sign the Minotaur's paper? He had never been one of the sporty boys at school who pushed their pain barriers. The interrogators would break him, like Zak—and probably quicker. The Minotaur would boast. *We have your friend's confession! He says you helped him. We can send you to jail for ten years at least. Think of your mother. . . .*

Moans, whimpers, shouts, and screams mingled with the new dull refrain, *What's the point?* Adam's head ached. It was the most terrible orchestra.

"I want to go home! I did nothing! I just want to go home!" He heard himself crying out loud.

"Who's making that racket in here?" The guard at the door glared into the cell. Zak stayed with his face to the wall as the guard faced Adam.

"You! Move it! You're wanted!"

Adam pushed himself off the bed. It was better not to have his arms yanked out by the guard. He kept his eyes on Zak, willing him to turn over. *Why won't you at least look at me? You got us into this!* But Zak remained motionless. Adam struggled to calm his breath. He was on his own.

IT'S NOT THE TRUTH!

THE MINOTAUR WAS LEANING BACK on his chair. He raised an eyebrow when Adam entered the interrogation room. The other two Permitteds watched in silence from behind their desks.

"So! You have had plenty of time to think what's best for you. Now you'll sign!" The Minotaur indicated to Adam to sit. His square face loomed forward as he placed a pen next to the piece of paper on the table. It was the statement typed in Permitted.

Later, Adam couldn't explain what happened to him except that it was like a sudden blast of trombones spurring him on. Grabbing the paper in front of him, he ripped it apart.

"It's not the truth." His voice trembled. The shredded pieces lay on the table between them. The Minotaur's eyes narrowed. Adam covered his head with his hands. What had he done?

A conversation followed with the other interrogators. It was about taking him to another room. In biology, they had learned how pain was felt in the brain. Could he empty his mind and make it blank? Would that help to stop feeling pain? He was still on the chair, next to the Minotaur's desk, when the telephone rang.

Another conversation, this time hurried, followed the phone call. It seemed that someone had arrived to attend his interrogation. The Minotaur, clearly irritated, swept the pieces of paper off his desk into a wastebasket. They weren't taking him to another room after all.

"Sit up!" he ordered Adam. "You have a visitor!"

Moments later, the visitor was ushered into the room. With her bush of gray hair and sharp brown eyes, Adam recognized the lawyer from the court. That day she only had time to tell Adam that his mother had asked her to help, and she would do her best. The lawyer's face was stern but lit up briefly to give Adam a quick smile.

"Good afternoon, Ms. Roth," the Minotaur muttered, pointing to a seat.

"I must first talk with my client." Her voice was crisp. "I haven't had the chance to speak with him yet." She spoke this last sentence in Non, switching from Permitted.

"You can speak to him later," said the Minotaur.

"No. It needs to be now and in private. It won't be as long as I've had to wait for you to inform me about his interrogation."

Adam could only half guess what they were saying in rapid Permitted. The Minotaur seemed twice the size of Ms. Roth, but she didn't seem afraid.

"Have you already asked him some questions?" Her voice cut the air in the room.

"Only a little talk," said the Minotaur, waving his hand as if it had been nothing.

Adam could tell that Ms. Roth wasn't pleased. She slowed the tempo of her words and he could now follow what she was saying. His interrogators had *broken* the rules. A *child of his age* should have a lawyer, or parent, with him during interrogation.

"So, now I must speak to my client before he answers *any further questions.*"

Adam held his breath. The Minotaur's silence felt like the moments before a huge storm. Then, to his surprise, the Minotaur nodded to the quiet interrogator, who signaled to Ms. Roth and Adam to follow him down the corridor. He opened the door to a room that was bare except for a table and two chairs. Was this the room from where the shrieks had escaped yesterday? Was this the room where Zak had been held?

Ms. Roth asked Adam to sit down and, as they waited for the door to close behind them, he decided he would tell her everything. Mama had asked this woman to speak for him in court. She was his only hope.

"They won't give us long," Ms. Roth began, now speaking only in Non. "Tell me what's happened to you."

His words came out in a jumble, beginning with Zak's crumpled body. He told her how Zak had signed a false statement, and they wanted Adam to confess that he gave Zak a knife—but there had been no knife! He had torn up the Minotaur's typed statement this morning—he hadn't planned to do that—and now they would stop Mama from getting her permit. If Ms. Roth hadn't come when she did, what would they be doing to him? What was going to happen now? Adam's head was throbbing.

Ms. Roth gazed directly at him. "You did the right thing, Adam," she declared firmly. "When someone confesses to something that's not true, it's much more difficult."

Adam's heart was racing. He tried to breathe deeply to make it slow down. With Ms. Roth in the room, the Minotaur would have to be more careful. But what would happen after she left? The lawyer seemed to read his thoughts.

"Stick to the truth, Adam. I'll do the very best I can."

"What will happen to Zak?"

"I'll do the very best I can for him too."

This time there was no forced standing on a spot; no bellowing, shouting, or screaming; no looming over him. Ms. Roth sat quietly beside him on the other side of the Minotaur's desk, making notes on her pad as the Minotaur tersely asked his questions. Adam repeated the same answers he had given before.

There wasn't a knife. I was carrying my violin case.

We slapped hands to say goodbye. That's all. There was no knife.

My friend likes to do tricks. Maybe those boys got scared but he jumped with his skateboard at the wall, not at them.

This time the Minotaur didn't type anything and there was no paper to sign. The Minotaur didn't look pleased when Ms. Roth declared that they had no evidence and Adam should be released. He couldn't follow everything, but it was obvious that the Minotaur didn't like being challenged by this fierce, small, gray-haired woman. An image popped into Adam's head of a furious bull, restrained by a rope, while a wiry little terrier snaps at its heels. He closed his eyes as the argument continued in Permitted.

Ms. Roth's voice, in Non, suddenly brought him back to the interrogation room. "We'll do everything we can, Adam. From what you have told me, you have no case to answer." She lowered her voice. "Stay with the truth. It will keep you strong."

The Minotaur called for an officer to take Adam away.

When Adam returned to his cell, Zak was no longer there. Where had they taken him? Adam was now sure that the Minotaur had ordered Zak to be brought to his cell as a warning.

This is what happens if you don't cooperate.

But now he had a new voice in his head.

Stay with the truth. It will keep you strong.

Ms. Roth had said what Dad would have said. It's what Mama and Grandma would also say. But could he be strong enough to keep with the truth if they did to him what they did to Zak? Dad was no longer here to protect him . . . and, even if he were still alive, what could Dad do? The only person on whom Adam could depend now was himself.

VOICES IN THE HEAD

ADAM WAITED ALONE IN HIS cell. Had the Minotaur finished his questions, or would he call Adam back? He soon began to lose track of time. The little square high above his bed turned dark at night and light in the morning . . . again and again. But he had no pen, no pencil, and nothing sharp enough to mark each day on the wall.

It's important to have a routine.

Dad's words. Why hadn't he asked Dad more about his time in a Permitted prison? Now it was too late, and he had only a few scraps of memories. Like one about Dad's musician friend who made a small flute out of a piece of old plastic tube. Dad's friend had found an iron nail and heated it to make holes in the tube. Dad said the melodies had cheered them on, reminding them of freedom.

Adam tried to keep his mind occupied. He imagined playing through all his scales and then every piece that he once knew by heart. Sometimes, he could only remember a fragment. That left him feeling more anxious, like failing a test. Then he would return to one of Grandma's favorite old Non melodies, which helped him relax. Yet however much he tried to stretch out his imaginary violin practice, the time seemed endless.

After imagining his violin practice, he tried listing the names of boys in his class, then the teachers at school and music school, followed by all the streets and places he knew in the Stone City. He imagined walking down a particular street and where that would take him. When his memory blurred, he was left upset and wracking his brain.

When his mind games grew tiresome, the thoughts from which he wanted to escape found their way back. He found himself thinking of details in the Minotaur's office and, when he couldn't stop those, images of Zak flooded in. He felt so helpless. What was happening to Zak now?

In the emptiness of his cell, Adam even began to wonder what it would be like if the Minotaur took him back to his office again. That way, he might at least find out more about his friend. He both wanted to know . . . and didn't. His mind flipped to the young archer's horse of power in his favorite folktale . . . *Sorry if you do, sorry if you don't.*

———

"Bring your things! Move it!"

The guard's scowl gave nothing away. Adam had nothing to bring except himself. His mind stalled as the guard hurried him out of the cell and toward the block with the Minotaur. But instead of being led to the Minotaur, the guard directed him to an office with a bunch of police officers clustered behind a long, high desk. His heart leaped when he recognized Ms. Roth on the other side of the desk.

"Hello, Adam!" Her voice was firm while the eyes behind her glasses smiled at him. "You are being released with no charges. My car is outside."

Adam struggled to absorb her words as Ms. Roth explained that she was taking him to her office. His mother would collect him from there.

It felt unreal to be outside . . . to feel sun on his face and a light breeze. The sudden colors confused him. A tree with bright red flowers on the other side of the street. Different shades of green on different trees and bushes. A yellow bird flitting from one branch to another. People walking on pavement and in passing cars. Did they know what happened behind those gray walls with their high barbed wire? Did they know that a boy who loved skateboarding could end up crumpled on a cell floor? By the time they reached Ms. Roth's car, Adam was fighting back tears.

Almost as soon as Ms. Roth started the engine, a cyclist

swung in front of them, balancing a stack of bread in his basket by the handlebar.

"Well, an acrobat!" she commented as Adam stared through the front window. It felt as if he was watching a film, not real life, here and now. Thank goodness Ms. Roth didn't expect him to say anything.

It wasn't long before Ms. Roth pulled up outside a green metal gate and tapped her car horn. The gate opened and she parked next to a large old building. As soon as they entered the shade of the entrance hall, a man with a drooping mustache hurried down a staircase, greeting them in Non.

"Ah, that's good you have at least one of them, Lily!"

Adam only half listened as Ms. Roth introduced her colleague as a friend of Zak's father. He needed his mother to come and take him home. *Home* . . . Figures in black swarmed into his head. One of them held up Grandfather's violin, ready to drop it. . . . His head was throbbing again. Where was Mama?

"Your mother won't be long," Ms. Roth said softly, pointing to a chair in her office. It was totally different from the Minotaur's room. Her bookshelves covered one whole wall. Previously, he would have wanted to look at the book titles. Today his eyes just roamed the pattern on the carpet. Scrolls of deep blue and scarlet reminded him of the scrolls on most violins. He wouldn't know until he got home if Grandfather's violin, with Little Jabari, was safe. What if the police had taken it away, saying that something might be hidden inside?

Ms. Roth's door opened. Adam sprang up from the chair into Mama's arms. As his head rocked against her shoulder, shudders rose from his stomach.

"I'll bring Adam back tomorrow. . . ."

"Good. The more he can tell us about Zak, the better we can defend him."

Ms. Roth's voice was quiet but clear. The nightmare wasn't over. While he was worrying whether the police had taken his violin, for all he knew, Zak might still be lying broken and crumpled in a cell.

Leila and Grandma stood under the front door's stone lintel, waiting for him. Mama had protected him from questions while he sat in silence at the back of Uncle Rami's car. He was dreading having to talk with Uncle Musa.

"Come, Adam." Grandma took his arm to lead him to the table. "I'm making your favorite omelet. Everything is prepared!"

"Please, Grandma . . ." Breaking his silence, he pried himself away.

"Give him a few minutes, Mother." Mama's voice dropped. "Zak's father will soon be here."

Adam darted past Leila to reach his bedroom. She had that desperate *Speak to me* look, yet all he could manage was a tiny nod. However, when she followed him, he couldn't bring himself to close the door on her. The violin case lay there on his bed. His fingers fumbled with the latches. As he opened the lid, Little Jabari's ears peeked up at him above the embroidered purple blanket. Catching his breath, he lifted the soft cloth and gazed. Grandfather Tomas's violin looked intact.

"Grandma found the blanket on the floor." Leila was leaning against the door frame, holding back from coming fully into the room. "She said those Permitteds had trampled on history! She even washed and ironed the cloth afterward. She was really upset."

Adam ran his fingers over the neat little blanket. It had always protected the violin, yet he had never asked about it. Was it Uncle Yosef's wife who had embroidered the cloth with this fine yellow thread? The young wife who had died . . .

Adam raised the violin and bow. First, he should tune each string, but the temptation was too strong. Instinctively, his bow found the right note and he began to play "We and the Moon Are Neighbors." With his eyes closed, he let Grandma's favorite Non melody carry him far away.

As he let the last note fade, he realized that Grandma was standing next to Leila at the bedroom door—and behind them was Mama with Zak's mother and father. Blood rose to his face. Zak's parents, Aunt Nadia and Uncle Musa, had found him playing the violin while Zak was still locked away.

"I'll make us some coffee," offered Mama.

"No, no, not for us, thank you," said Uncle Musa.

"We just want to ask Adam if he saw Zak in the prison. How is he?" Aunt Nadia clasped her hands together as if praying.

She kept them like that even after everyone sat down. Mama sat close to Adam on the settee. He felt her support, but how could he explain what it was like inside there with the Minotaur? Or find words for his friend curled up and sobbing on the cell floor? He couldn't bring himself to tell Zak's parents that their son had signed a false confession, although they probably already knew from Ms. Roth. All he could do was simply say yes or no to their questions, or stay silent. He couldn't bear to look up into their eyes.

After a few minutes, Mama said it would be best to let Adam rest. They would go to see Ms. Roth with Uncle Musa in the morning. It was vital for Adam to give the lawyer any information that could help Zak. That would be the most useful thing. Uncle Musa agreed.

As Mama accompanied Zak's parents to the front door, their voices turned into murmurs. Adam remained seated, vaguely aware of Grandma calling Leila to help her. Without warning, the Minotaur's voice jumped into his head, so close and loud it was like he was beside him. *We know EVERYTHING ABOUT YOU!* Adam covered his ears, threw his head on his knees. *Your mother is waiting for a new permit, isn't she?*

He needed his violin to escape this voice in his head! But as he pushed himself up from the settee, he felt Grandma's fingers firmly circling his arm.

"Come, Adam. Your omelet is ready." The warmth in Grandma's hand and her familiar voice broke the spell. "I'm sure you didn't have anything good to eat inside that terrible place." She led Adam to the table. A sunny omelet and salad dishes, colorful as flowers in a field, made him aware of pangs in his stomach. For the time being, the Minotaur was banished.

Grandma had made omelets for everyone. No one asked him any more questions. Mama kept the conversation to Grandma's magic touch with eggs and asking Leila about school. Adam let the conversation drift around him until he heard Mama ask Leila about music school. Did they have a date yet for the summer concert? Leila thought it was a date early in June. Adam's mind whirled.

"What day is it now?" He surprised himself by speaking.

"First of May," said Mama, smiling at him. Grandma and Leila smiled too. He needed to absorb what that meant. He'd had a plan, hadn't he? He had to stop Mama from being sent away. The concert was in June—only a month away. That wasn't long! He would have to work really hard to be ready. Any interruptions would set him back. How could he keep out the images and voices that kept invading his head?

Zak on his cell floor . . . Zak saying what they had done to him . . . Zak signing a false confession . . . The Minotaur screaming in Zak's face . . .

If Ms. Roth hadn't arrived at the police station just in time, he was sure they would have done to him what they did to Zak. The tears began to run down Adam's cheeks. The salad on his plate was a blur. He was shaking and sobbing. Mama was leaning over, trying to wrap him in her arms again. But this time the dam had burst.

TRAPPED

THE NEXT MORNING, ADAM SAT between Mama and Uncle Musa, opposite Ms. Roth in her office. He kept his eyes focused on the desk ahead as the adults talked. He stared at a photograph of a girl in a silver frame next to a pile of papers. He hadn't noticed it the day before. There was something about her direct gaze and quite cheeky hairstyle that reminded him of Leila. Adam tried to concentrate on what the adults were saying. He had seen how fierce Ms. Roth could be, standing up to the Minotaur. When she turned to Adam, her voice was firm yet gentle, although her questions were soon leading him into a jungle of shadows and monsters. He could feel Mama and Uncle Musa willing him on. For Zak's sake—for all their sakes—he had to remember everything and say it out loud. The sound of Ms. Roth tapping on her keyboard was at least reassuring and quite different from the sound of the Minotaur's keyboard.

It was, however, when he came to describing how Zak had been made to sit for hours bent over on a low stool that words deserted Adam. Suddenly he was trying to explain through gestures, twisting his hands and arms behind his back. Ms. Roth nodded as if to say that she understood. It seemed she had heard about such unspeakable things before.

Adam's words returned. "Zak signed their paper. He told me . . . but he only guessed what it said . . . it was in Permitted." Ms. Roth's fingers tapped on a few seconds more.

"Thank you, Adam," she said at last. "This is very helpful. Well done." Mama gently patted his shoulder, but Uncle Musa was silent. He had covered his eyes with one hand.

"I'm sorry—but it happens," said Ms. Roth. "This is very hard for your family and, of course, for Zak."

Uncle Musa slowly wiped his face as Ms. Roth began to explain. With Zak having signed a statement, the prosecution might want to delay his court case until he turned fourteen, when he could be sent to a prison for adults. If the judge found him guilty, Zak could then be given a longer sentence.

"How long?" Uncle Musa's question was like a low growl of pain.

Ms. Roth paused. She opened her palms and cupped

her hands as if measuring something invisible. "I can't say for sure. A fourteen-year-old Non boy recently got twelve years. His charge was attempted murder. That's probably the charge Zak will face."

Attempted murder! Adam felt numb. He listened as Ms. Roth explained that Zak had a harsh choice. Instead of risking the delay and a longer sentence, he could agree now to plead guilty in return for a lighter sentence. She called it a "plea bargain."

"But it's not the truth!" Adam blurted out. Hadn't he torn up the Minotaur's paper, saying the very same words? Didn't Ms. Roth also tell him to stick with the truth when the Minotaur interviewed him in her presence?

"I know." Ms. Roth looked solemnly at him. He returned her gaze. "However, this is now different. The police have a statement signed by Zak. I can imagine it says that he *wanted* to attack the Permitted boys. Of course, when he gets to court, he can say that he was forced to sign a false statement—and he can tell the judge what they did to him. But the police will deny this. They will say he's lying. Even if you appear as his witness, Adam, will the judge believe you and your friend Zak? Or will they believe the police and the Permitted boys who say he attacked them?" Once again, Ms. Roth spread her palms wide open. It looked like a plea, although Adam didn't know to whom.

Rage rose like a sudden storm inside him. Zak was trapped. His family was trapped. They were all trapped, weren't they? The Minotaur and other Permitteds like him ruled over a giant maze in which Nons were snared. What use was truth when everything was set up to trap them?

"I want to go!" Adam pushed back his chair. "I'll wait downstairs." Mama lurched to restrain him, but Uncle Musa put out an arm, shielding him.

"Let him go. He needs some air," said Uncle Musa. Adam grabbed the handle of Ms. Roth's door and fled.

RETURN TO THE PLAN

"YOU NEED TO GET BACK to school and your old routine. It'll help," Mama announced while they were eating dinner.

Adam knew she was referring to his outburst in Ms. Roth's office earlier in the day. On the way home from the lawyer's office, the silence in Uncle Rami's taxi had been broken by Zak's father. Adam had wondered if his words were meant especially for him. "This lawyer knows what she's talking about. We must trust her. We have no choice. We must go for this plea bargain—and pray Zak's sentence isn't too long."

Did Uncle Musa think he had been angry at Ms. Roth? But that wasn't it! He was angry at the trap that Zak was in—that *all* Nons were in! How would going back to school and his old routine change that? The power Permitteds held over Nons was so unfair! Yet Uncle Musa and even Mama were saying they had "no choice" but to carry on.

Once again, as in Ms. Roth's office, Adam felt a surge of rage. He felt like abandoning dinner for his room when Grandma reached for his hand. The touch of her fingers restrained him.

"What your mother is really saying, Adam, is 'Don't give up hope!'" Grandma spoke softly. "If you go straight back to school, you will show they haven't beaten you. Instead, let your bad experiences make you stronger."

Her words reminded him of something Dad used to say when asked about his work in archaeology: *Our people have survived here for hundreds and hundreds of years. If the Permitteds think they can force us to give up our hope of dignity and equality in our land, they will fail.*

Adam remained silent. His anger was no longer bubbling and bursting, but it was still there inside him. Deep down, he knew that when the adults spoke about carrying on, they weren't giving up or giving in. When he finally managed to look directly at Mama, she responded with an encouraging smile. However, as she began to discuss the next day's arrangements, he thought he saw a hint of tears.

Mama said she would accompany him to school in the morning and speak with the principal. After school, Adam should collect Leila and continue to music school together. Mr. B had been keeping in touch with Mama and they were now all looking forward to seeing Adam again. After music school, Adam and Leila must walk straight back home. They must, of course, use the Northwest Gate. Mama didn't need to say why.

Adam got through his first day back at school by keeping himself inside his bubble and hardly speaking. He could tell the other boys had been told to give him space. Yet some kept hanging around and he knew they wanted to ask about the prison. That's why he needed his bubble. If it burst, how could he control what would come out?

After school, Leila's eyes lit up on seeing Adam. She ran from her school gate toward him, flute case bouncing in one hand. He was aware of curious glances from other children, and he wondered whether she had been pestered with questions about him. But Leila was always chattier, so maybe she didn't mind.

They had just crossed the busy road that led to Uncle Mikhail's bookshop when Leila turned to ask, "Did you hear my flute in the court?"

Adam nodded. It helped that there were some things she already knew, like the court, the police raid on their house . . . But he still didn't want to talk, and quickened his pace.

"We don't want to be late," he mumbled. It was safer staying inside his bubble.

Adam was relieved when Mr. B said very simply, "We're glad to have you back, Adam. With a month to the concert, there's a lot to do—but you can do it."

After tuning the strings, he began his old routine, starting with his scales. His fingers were stiff, and he stumbled a few times, yet Mr. B let him proceed to Vivaldi's "Spring." Normally, when he made a mistake, Mr. B would stop and make him repeat, but today Mr. B was giving him time to get back into his stride.

Adam glanced at Little Jabari. They should be riding through a valley in spring! Yet he could only feel tight and tense with no pleasure in hearing bird trills or water bubbling in a stream.

It was only when he began making rapid bows for the storm that he briefly felt at one with the music. But instead of imagining thunder and lightning, suddenly Zak flashed through his mind, streaking downhill, hurling his skateboard up at a wall. Adam gripped his bow so tight that his right hand seized up. His left hand clutched Little Jabari as he stood silent, feeling helpless.

"Sit down . . . please sit down, Adam." Mr. B's hand steered him to a chair. He let Mr. B take his violin and bow and place them on his desk. Adam sank his head into his hands. How on earth had he thought he could be ready in time for the concert? His plan to stop Mama from being deported was wrecked.

"Come, have this." Mr. B had poured Adam a glass of water. His teacher pulled up a chair next to him. "After what you've been through, Adam, you need to give yourself more time."

"I *have* to do this, Mr. B," Adam whispered. He forced himself to look up at his teacher. His eyes were pricking but he was determined not to let loose any tears.

"Well, there's still a month, and we can see how you go. Don't be so hard on yourself. There will be other concerts and chances in the future."

I won't be here, thought Adam. *If the Permitteds send Mama over the Wall, Leila and I will have to go with her . . . and we won't be able to come to our music school anymore!* He stood up, ready to pick up his violin and bow again. Mr. B raised the palm of his hand.

"First, you have to relax," he insisted. "Copy me."

It was like going back to basics again . . . breathing in and out very slowly, then shaking out the muscles in his hands and arms. Afterward, Mr. B checked his posture.

"Your violin is part of you. It feels what you feel."

Adam nodded. He was ready to try the Vivaldi again. He would think only of the notes and the music. But Mr. B surprised him.

"Let's play something different. Vivaldi can wait." Picking up his own violin and bow, Mr. B began an old Non melody that Adam knew by heart. The rhythm seeped into him, his foot began to tap, and he raised his bow. He had to concentrate on keeping up with Mr. B, but once he was inside the music, there was nothing else. When the melody ended and their last notes faded, Mr. B murmured, "That was beautiful. It would have made your grandfather very happy."

Adam's lips tightened as he tried to say "Thank you." He hoped that Mr. B understood.

There had been nothing to smile about for the past terrible weeks, and Zak was probably going to prison for a long time. But it was also true that this old Non melody was very beautiful . . . and he had helped to bring it alive.

He made a silent wish. There was still time to bring Vivaldi's springtime valley alive in the concert. He *had* to carry through with his plan to save Mama from being deported.

Adam was taking out his violin in his bedroom when he heard Uncle Musa's voice. He immediately put the violin on his bed and entered the sitting room. Uncle Musa looked as if he hadn't slept for days.

"They moved Zak from the central police station but won't say where they have taken him! They say we can't see him until his trial!" Mama and Grandma shook their heads in sympathy.

"There's nothing we can do . . . except wait and wait." According to Ms. Roth, the police often did this.

"They want to punish us, the family, as well!" he added grimly.

Mama poured Uncle Musa a cup of coffee and Adam slipped away to his bedroom. He wanted to start practicing, but with Zak's father in the house, he felt awkward. Instead, he looked for Uncle Elias's book. The last time he had written anything in it was before the police raid. That was just a week ago, but it seemed much, much longer. What had Uncle Elias said? *Write what you are feeling, thinking.* He found his book and a pen. He would play his violin when Uncle Musa left.

IF ONLY I'D SAID YES . . .

Zak, you wanted me
to take my turn
on your skateboard.
I said no,
we were already late.
If only I'd said yes,
we'd never have seen those boys
coming up the hill.
You'd have never set off
on that last mad ride on your skateboard.
You'd still be here.
I want to turn back the clock
and say yes, yes, yes!
I want my turn on your skateboard!
You can teach me
to ollie
to nollie
and all your tricks!
If only I'd said yes.

THE PARAKEET AND THE FLAG

ADAM AND LEILA RETURNED TO their morning routine of Mama waving them off to school and watching them set off for the Northwest Gate. Neither said anything, but each kept an eye out for groups of young Permitteds. Even without Mama telling them, there was no question about coming home through the busy Great Gate and the alleys.

A week later, however, after music school, as they came through the Northwest Gate, instead of continuing straight ahead, Leila pointed to a smaller street on their left. Adam knew where it would lead.

"Can we go home this way and say hello to the parakeet? I want to see if he remembers us!" Leila gave Adam her eyes-wide-open look.

Adam was about to say, "No, it's where the Permitteds

took Aunt Hala's house!" but stopped himself. There were no longer demonstrations and police guards. Why shouldn't they walk that way? The alley didn't belong to the Permitteds, and most of the houses still belonged to Nons. Even though he didn't want to bump into Zak's chief accuser, it would be cowardly to avoid the alley just because of him.

"All right, but we won't stop for long."

The alley was empty, and the parakeet was still there in its cage on the window ledge. Leila skipped up to it. She made little clicking noises. The parakeet cocked its head and copied her. Adam couldn't help smiling and began to make different clicks for the bird to copy. It was such fun that he took no interest in Leila assembling her flute until she lifted it to her lips. She blew a few notes that sounded like a bird. Both children waited. Puffing out its cheeks, the excited parakeet ran up and down its wooden perch. When Leila repeated the notes, it became even more excited. The third time, the parakeet let out a trill.

"He's answering!" She laughed and Adam joined her. "He's been missing us and—" Leila's voice froze. Adam followed her gaze. Two Permitted boys, one older and one younger, had appeared around the bend in the alley and were walking in their direction. The older was Zak's accuser, and it was obvious that he recognized them too. After a moment's hesitation, the sandy-haired teenager took the small boy by the hand, continuing toward them. Leila deliberately lifted her flute and, turning her back, played again for the parakeet. Her notes sounded more defiant this time. Adam stood facing the alley, determined not to show his anxiety. His eyes veered between Leila, the parakeet, and the boys coming toward them. His mouth felt dry.

The older boy was walking more quickly now, hurrying the child, who looked like a younger brother. It suddenly dawned on Adam that the teenager was nervous. Without his friends, he didn't look so bold and arrogant. Instead, he kept his eyes fixed on the ground while the small boy's eyes darted toward Leila and the parakeet. There was no chance of the child being allowed to stop and watch. What did these young Permitteds think he and Leila would do to them?

As soon as the pair had passed, the front door opened. It was the parakeet's owner. The lady's sharp eyes took in everything—Leila with her flute, Adam standing alert, and the Permitted boys heading up the alley. When her eyes returned to Leila, her face creased into a smile.

"Thank you for playing for my little friend! Please wait a minute," she said, and disappeared into her house. Adam sighed. Why had he agreed to this diversion? Just because Mr. B had said "very good," it didn't mean he could take things easy! Leila put away her flute and was waving goodbye to the parakeet when its owner returned with a plate of cookies. She insisted they each take a couple. They thanked her and hurried down the alley.

As soon as they reached the bend, they saw the Permitted flag. It hung out over the alley, attached to a long pole from an upstairs window of Aunt Hala's house. It wasn't enough that a Non family had been evicted. The new inhabitants were announcing it boldly to their Non neighbors with their flag. Grandma would say "rubbing salt into the wound." The alley was quiet, but the flag was a stark reminder of Aunt Hala's green-velvet settee, carpets, pots, pans, and everything else thrown into the alley—as well as the protestors, the police. Adam could still hear the Permitted father's voice: *What's a Non boy like you doing with a beautiful violin like this?*

Adam clenched the handle of his violin case, recalling the clang of stones hitting Aunt Hala's pans with Zak's scream of "Stop, thief!" He was aware of Leila staring up at the water tank on the rooftop opposite the alley. Was she also thinking about Zak? Together they hurried, in silence, past the flag, toward the street that led home.

THE BUBBLE BURSTS

FOR THE NEXT THREE WEEKS, Adam thought only about the concert. There were no more diversions. At school he kept himself in his bubble. At home, as soon as he finished his homework, he closed the door of his bedroom and practiced the first movement of Vivaldi's "Spring." For hours he repeated phrases over and over, until he could imagine Mr. B saying, "Good." Then he would continue to the next few bars and try to perfect them, although he still couldn't imagine Mr. B saying, "Bellissimo."

Mr. B responded to Adam's effort with extra lessons, and he accompanied him on the piano. He showed Adam a short poem by Vivaldi. It was only eight lines.

Spring has arrived.
Birds celebrate with a happy song.

Streams stroked by little breezes
Flow softly with sweet murmurs.
A black cloak swathes the sky.
Thunder and lightning proclaim a storm.
Then die to silence and, once again,
Birds sing their lovely song.

"Thank you, Mr. B," said Adam, "but I prefer the music."

"So do I!" declared Mr. B. "Vivaldi was a musician! If you bring these pictures alive as you play, that will indeed be poetry."

Adam understood. Yet he couldn't explain to Mr. B that it wasn't spring in just *any* valley. This had to be the valley of family picnics below the hillside outside the Stone City where Dad would take them every year in spring . . . where Grandma told stories of the long, wide valley of her family's home in the Time Before . . . where Adam imagined Grandfather Tomas as a boy riding freely on the real Jabari . . . where Great-Grandfather and Uncle Yosef made music together in the family house . . . until the arrival of the Permitteds with guns. His violin with its Little Jabari, handmade and played by Uncle Yosef, knew that valley in the Time Before. Now it was up to him to make it sing.

Even when he wasn't practicing, Adam let the music play in his head. It surrounded him in his bubble. He wanted to learn the whole first movement by heart so he wouldn't need his sheet music. Mama began to complain that it was driving her mad having to repeat herself to get his attention. Adam still revealed nothing about his plan. The music became a shield. If thoughts of the Minotaur, or even Zak, tried to slip into his head, he replaced them with the rumble of thunder, rapidly repeating the same note. His imaginary bow and his fingers would slide up the scale like lightning. The storm would end in silence and, holding his breath, he would wait for the birdsong to return.

In his final lesson before the concert, Adam played the whole first movement. Twice he stumbled, but Mr. B said nothing and let him continue. Adam knew it was a test to see if he would recover. A glance at Little Jabari was enough to remind him that he could. When he drew his bow slowly down on the final note, he closed his eyes to wait for his teacher's verdict. If Mr. B didn't think his playing was good enough, he would tell Adam to delay until the next concert. But if Mama's permission had already been refused, they would no longer be living in the Stone City.

Mr. B slowly raised his fingers away from the piano. "You'll be fine," he said. "Your grandfather would be content to hear you play his violin with such feeling."

Adam felt a burst of relief. It took a couple of deep breaths to focus on Mr. B's advice. He should get a good night's sleep and include time to relax before tomorrow evening's concert. Could he get the afternoon off school? Adam said he would ask his mother. Then, shyly, he asked Mr. B, "Will the famous violinist be coming from OverSeas?"

Mr. B assured him that she had arrived safely and would be there. "But don't let nerves get in the way, Adam. Just play with your heart. Play like you did today!"

Adam nodded while his stomach tightened. If he didn't impress the famous violinist, his plan was useless.

Despite Leila's pleas, Adam walked even faster than usual after music school to get home with his news.

"Mama already knows you're good enough for the concert!" she protested.

"How can you say that?" retorted Adam. "*I* didn't know!"

It was true. He really hadn't been sure he could learn the whole piece in time. Even now, he was intending to practice at least a couple of hours after dinner. He didn't want to repeat the mistakes he had made playing for Mr. B.

As they came up the steps to their house, Adam saw that Zak's father was at the open door. He looked agitated and on the point of leaving, but he was still talking.

"Let me know who is coming. We'll see how many Rami can take in his car."

Adam and Leila stood aside to let Uncle Musa pass. He was so distracted that he gave no greeting. Mama appeared and ushered them in.

"Zak's trial is tomorrow," she said bluntly as soon as

they stepped inside. "His family heard only an hour ago. They want to know if we'd like to attend." Her voice was as somber as her eyes.

Adam felt his bubble burst. His concert was also tomorrow! He flung himself onto the settee, leaving Leila to tell his news. Mama attempted a smile but his good news was ruined. How could it be good when, on the same day, Zak was going to be sent to prison for years on a false charge? Adam had tried so hard to banish upsetting thoughts of Zak and the Minotaur . . . and now this! How could he relax as Mr. B had advised? He remained too choked up to speak until he heard Mama say, "With your concert tomorrow evening, perhaps it's better if you don't go to the court, Adam."

"But I have to go! I want to see Zak! It'll be my only chance for . . . for . . ." His voice trailed off. For how many years would Zak be sent to prison?

Grandma had been sitting at the table, listening. She looked up at Mama. "He's young. I'm sure he'll manage both," she said quietly. She turned to Adam, hunched over his violin case. "When Zak's all alone, he will remember you came. It will help him." Her words lingered in the silent room.

"It's your decision," said Mama after a few moments. "But do you think you can manage the concert after going to the court?"

Adam forced himself to sit up straight. He *had* to

continue with the concert. Only he knew just why it was so important. At the same time, he *had* to see Zak. He *had* to manage both . . . like Grandma said he could.

"Yes," he said in a voice little more than a whisper. "I will."

Adam was finishing his dinner when a headache gripped his skull. It pressed inward, making him wince. Leila saw and gave her special wide-eyed look. He drew his right arm across his eyes, hoping it looked like he was just wiping away some irritation. Luckily, Leila didn't say anything and neither Mama nor Grandma noticed. He excused himself, taking his plate to the sink before escaping to his bedroom.

Cradling Little Jabari in the palm of his left hand, Adam willed the headache to let go and told his fingers to relax. Instead, the pain made his left hand grip even more tightly around the scroll and his right fingers around the bow. It was pointless trying to play like this! Maybe if he went to sleep early, he could fit in a short practice when he was fresh in the morning, before they set off for the court?

In the bathroom, he found Mama's bottle of aspirin on the top shelf of the medicine cabinet and quickly swallowed a couple with a glass of water. She would be upset that he was taking them without her knowledge. But after her doubts about him attending Zak's case, he couldn't risk telling her.

Snatches of melody from Vivaldi came to mind as Adam drifted into sleep. He imagined he was lying down in the grass of his grandparents' valley. It was peaceful. But in the middle of the night, he woke with his teeth clenched. The Minotaur was somewhere in the dark of his room. Seized with fear, he pulled the duvet over his head. How had the Minotaur entered so silently? Had he come to force Adam back into prison with Zak? Adam's heart beat so loudly, the sound would surely give him away.

In the end, he could bear it no longer. Slipping his hand from under the duvet, he flipped on his bedside light and sat up. He was alone, trembling. There was no one else in the room. Grandfather's violin lay in its open case just where he had left it when his head had been wracking with pain. Adam sank forward on the bed, arms around his ribs, trying to steady his breathing. How foolish! Of course, it had just been a nightmare. Yet it was a little while before he felt able to turn off his light, lie down again, and close his eyes.

Instead of waking early to practice, he only woke when Mama knocked loudly on his door. Time to get up! They would have a quick breakfast before setting off for the court. Uncle Rami was going to make a couple of trips. Everyone in both families was coming, including Zak's grandmother.

Only Grandma said she would stay at home, as she

needed to reserve her energy for Adam's concert later. She would be thinking of Zak all the time and, if they could speak with him, they must give him her message: "Never lose hope."

TWO RAISED THUMBS

THE COURT CORRIDORS WERE ALREADY crowded with families when they arrived. The air was hot and stuffy. Everyone seemed to be waiting for a court number to be called. Adam tried hard to create a new bubble for himself. He was terrified for Zak and, at the same time, also wanted to run through his piece. Maybe it would calm him too. Yet as soon as he began to hear the music inside his head, a loudspeaker voice would break both the melody and his bubble.

Later, Ms. Roth, who had been talking with Zak's parents, came to ask how he was doing. Adam let Mama speak for him. Ms. Roth's face had that tired smile he had seen before. However, when Mama mentioned his concert, her eyes lit up.

"I'd love to attend," she said. "Music helps to revive me." After asking Mama about the time and place, she disappeared down the corridor.

Leila poked Adam gently with her finger. "Do you know that Ms. Roth saved my flute?" She explained how the court usher had wanted to take away her flute after she had played it to get his attention inside the courtroom.

"Mmm . . ." was all Adam managed. It was impossible to practice anything in his head here and his dread for Zak was growing by the minute, alongside his impatience to have everything over and done. The Permitteds in charge thought they could keep Nons waiting forever.

When Zak's case was finally called, they all hurried after Uncle Musa. They were just in time to see Zak brought into the courtroom, handcuffed and surrounded by four police guards. Then Adam noticed Zak was shuffling. They had even shackled his feet! Did they think he could fly away?

The guards led Zak past his family so quickly that the chains were cutting into his ankles and he was tottering. When Zak's mother stretched out her fingers to touch him, her hand landed instead on the arm of a guard. The policeman spun around, as if under attack. Zak tried to look back but was pushed forward. Aunt Nadia beat her hand against her heart. "My love!" she cried out while Zak's grandmother did her best to comfort her.

A glimpse of Zak's face close-up was enough for Adam

to recognize the barrier across his friend's dark eyes. Hadn't he also tried to hide inside himself when brought into the Permitteds' court? The memory flooded back of how small he had felt when surrounded by police. The guards who now blocked Zak from the people who loved him knew that he couldn't threaten them. They were just showing off their power over a Non boy . . . a boy who loved skateboarding and who hated bullies. Adam's eyes anxiously scoured the court for the Minotaur. Even though Adam couldn't see him, it felt like his shadow was hovering.

The case was over in minutes. Uncle Musa held his head in both hands, repeating in a monotone, "Three years . . . three years!" Zak would be sixteen before Adam could see him again. The Permitted judge had just taken away three years of Zak's life! Adam felt his stomach twist at the unfairness of it all.

Almost immediately, the guards prepared to march his friend out of the courtroom. Zak was desperately trying to turn around to see his family. A moment later, he was being hauled away. Without warning, Zak jerked his head back. At the same time, he managed to lift his handcuffs to show two raised thumbs. It was the sign he would make before setting off on his skateboard, to say "I'm ready." The gesture now was defiant.

Adam headed straight to his bedroom, leaving Mama and Leila to tell Grandma everything. The distress of seeing

Zak dragged away left him so angry that he was in no state to practice for his concert. Yet his whole plan to stop Mama from being sent over the Wall depended on his performance tonight! Even if he could calm himself, the concert now seemed impossible. He would be drained and useless.

Mama had been right after all. He shouldn't have gone to the court. All he could manage was to crawl into bed and shut down his mind.

Adam must have fallen asleep because he woke with a start, knowing someone was in his room. He felt a moment of fright until he saw Grandma shuffling toward him. She lowered herself carefully and sat silently near him on the bed, placing her aged hand on top of his.

Adam said nothing but just listened to her breaths . . . Largo. He could hear Mr. B explaining: *Long. Even. Measured.*

"You'll play beautifully this evening," Grandma said. Her voice was a soft, smooth legato, her eyes resting on his. "I wish your grandfather could hear how you make his violin sing! Also Uncle Yosef, who made it . . ." She paused. "But it really is *your* violin now. Your father would be so proud of you. We all are . . . and I believe that goes for Zak too . . ." She paused again. "Leila told me how he raised his thumbs."

Adam squeezed Grandma's hand. He wasn't going to try to speak. Using both hands to push herself up, Grandma limped away from the bed. But instead of heading to the door, she made her way to his bookcase, where his violin case lay open on the top shelf. She hobbled back to Adam with the instrument resting in her arms. She laid it in front of him and eased herself down again.

"There's something I never fully explained about your grandfather." Grandma's eyes shifted between Adam and the violin. "I told you that he named this Little Jabari, but there was also something else."

Adam sat up, now fully alert.

"I think my Tomas was embarrassed in case I thought he was being childish when he was a grown man." Grandma's eyes lit up for a moment. "He told me how sometimes, when he was playing, he imagined he was on the back of my father's best stallion, the *real* Jabari, in their old valley. The two of them would dance together over the hills, just the two of them, quite free and happy. He even told me not to be jealous!"

Adam understood perfectly. Even for his grandfather, freedom was a dream. "It wasn't childish, was it, Grandma?"

"No, Adam. It wasn't," she said simply. "Without our dreams, what are we?" She stretched a hand across the bed. Her fingers touched the violin's scroll. "After we fled, your grandfather had to give up working with horses and riding freely through our valley . . . but Little Jabari and this violin reminded him. In fact, they kept his dream alive."

Alarm bells suddenly rang for Adam. He jerked upright and checked his watch. His concert was in less than three hours and he hadn't practiced at all today!

"I must do my final practice now, Grandma!"

Grandma must have heard the panic in his voice. She smiled gently. "You'll be fine, don't worry," she said, raising herself again carefully from the bed. "You have Little Jabari with you, don't you?"

Adam flushed. What did Grandma know? She couldn't possibly have guessed his secret plan and why his performance was so important for their family. Moreover, he felt far from fine.

"You must eat something before we leave. Don't be too long," Grandma advised before shutting the door quietly behind her.

“SPRING”

WEDGED BETWEEN MAMA AND LEILA in the back of the taxi, Adam cradled his violin case. Grandma had recognized the driver, and, sitting next to him, was asking all about his family. Outside, the noise increased as they entered the main street outside the Stone City while Adam tried to conjure a picture of a peaceful valley. It was impossible to filter out the rumbling of traffic, engines revving, hooting, door slamming, and shouts. At least in music school, he could retreat somewhere to tune his strings and practice a few scales.

The first thing Adam saw as they turned the final corner were two police cars parked outside the music school’s gate. The taxi pulled up behind them and Mama climbed out of the car to help Grandma. A mixture of fear and anger seized Adam.

"We have to get out, Adam!" Leila urged. But his body had frozen. Were the police coming back for him? The taxi driver turned to see what was happening.

"Is the seat belt stuck?"

Adam forced his head to shake no. The movement seemed to unlock his body and, mechanically, he edged out of the car.

"What's wrong, Adam?" Mama asked after she had paid the driver. His face felt hot as he stared blankly at the nearest police car. Mama suddenly understood. She had that look of wanting to put her arm around him, but Grandma was clutching on to her.

"It's all right," Mama said in her soft but firm voice. "Their cars are everywhere. They aren't coming for you. They may just have parked here and gone over the road or around the corner."

"I hope they haven't gone to Uncle Mikhail's bookshop!" Leila exclaimed.

Mama raised her eyebrows. "You too, Leila; stay calm, please. It's been a difficult day for everyone, but Adam's concert will lift all our spirits."

Grandma was already peering over the gate. "It's good to see this lovely old house again. It's a fine place to play your violin, Adam."

Mama's and Grandma's composure helped Adam shift his thoughts away from the police cars as they entered the courtyard. The limestone walls of the music school looked like they were bathed in golden honey. Grandma often remarked how she loved seeing such old stones turn rosy at sunset. Clicking the gate behind them, Adam shut out the street.

The butterflies in his stomach were flapping crazily as Adam waited among the performers in the courtyard. The audience was on the other side of a temporary stage in front of the building. Because they were early, Grandma, Mama, and Leila had even found seats in the front row alongside the seats reserved for special visitors. Would they be near the famous violinist from OverSeas? Glancing at the front row, Adam couldn't tell who it was. Why hadn't he checked out her photograph? He also looked for Ms. Roth but couldn't see her. Maybe she wouldn't come after all.

Yet whoever was in the audience, he had to do his very best. Mr. B had said that Adam's Vivaldi was to be the final piece. *We want the audience to go away with hope, isn't that so, Adam?* In the meantime, he had to quiet the maddening butterflies.

As darkness fell, the stage lights took over, leaving the audience in shadow. Adam allowed his mind to empty, losing himself in the sounds . . . traveling wherever the music of the performers took him. His violin lay on his lap. Little Jabari in his left hand helped to calm him. However, when four students with Non instruments began playing a joyful dance, the rhythm touched him so deep down that every fiber of his body felt alive. He even wanted to raise Little Jabari and join in! How Dad would have loved the Non melodies and drumming! For a few moments he imagined his father clapping with the audience as the refrain pulsed through the courtyard.

But at the end of the applause, Adam hurtled into doubts. How could he capture the audience like that? The next piece was already being announced. He heard the words "by the composer Elgar." Didn't Mr. B say this was his cue? He would be next! Pinned to his seat as if by an arrow, he listened to the cello, viola, and violins soar in a melody so sad that his eyes began to prick. In a flash, his mind was back into prison with Zak sobbing on the cell floor. Adam pressed his lips together and clutched Little Jabari so tightly that the wooden ears dug into his palm.

Hold on, son . . . hold on. Dad's voice came as a deep bass. Just in time.

Slowly, he breathed in . . . *hold, two, three, four* . . . breathed out . . . *hold, two, three, four* . . . Relaxing his grip on the little chestnut horse, Adam looked up at the night sky, already a deep indigo. There was a sliver of new moon. It was the same sky above Zak, wherever he was, even if he couldn't see it. This same sky also stretched over the valley where Grandfather once rode the real chestnut Jabari. As the music soared again, Adam recalled Zak's last gesture.

Adam's thumbs rose by themselves. He and Little Jabari would take the audience so they too could hear the birds singing freely . . . see a flash of emerald calling "Follow! Follow!" . . . and feel all creatures waking in the spring!

From the piano, Mr. B offered a quick reassuring smile to Adam as he stepped onto the stage. After a final tuning of his strings, Adam closed his eyes to let Vivaldi's opening notes enter his head. He and Little Jabari were ready to fly into their valley.

Afterward, Adam had to wait for the applause to die down. There were calls of "Encore!" Mr. B was smiling and nodding to him to give the audience a short encore. But if he didn't speak to them now, he might lose his chance. He raised his bow and stepped forward. There was a hush. With his timpani heart thumping, Adam spoke as clearly and loudly as possible.

"Thank you. When I play 'Spring' by Vivaldi, it reminds me of my grandfather. He loved horses when he was my age. He used to ride freely through the valley and over the hills outside the Stone City. That was in the Time Before. My grandfather gave me this violin and it's really special because it has a horsehead for the scroll." Adam held up Little Jabari. "It was handmade by Uncle Yosef . . . a Permitted friend of our family. He gave it as a present for my grandfather when our family had to flee from the other

Permitteds who were coming with guns. My grandma told me . . . and she is here tonight."

Murmurs rippled through the audience until Adam held up his bow again. He hadn't finished.

"Tonight, I played especially for my mother. She's here with Grandma and my sister, Leila, who also loves our music school. Mama has been waiting for her permit to stay with us in the Stone City. We are very worried that she may be sent away over the Wall. What will happen to our family?"

Cries of "Shame!" and "Disgraceful!" broke out. Once again, Adam indicated he hadn't finished.

"Tonight, I'm also playing for my friend Zak. He loves skateboarding, but today he was sent to prison for three years for something he didn't do. . . ."

Adam heard his voice tremble. For a dreadful moment, he was alarmed he would lose control. Then he felt Mr. B's hand rest on his shoulder.

"But my grandma says we mustn't give up hope and we must keep our dreams alive."

The audience was silent and for the first time since coming onto the stage, Adam tried to see into the audience. He still couldn't identify the famous violinist, but suddenly everyone began clapping again and then he heard "Bravo, Adam!" He recognized the voice. It was Ms. Roth. As his eyes adjusted, he made her out just behind Leila. A girl who looked the same as the one in the picture on Ms. Roth's desk was sitting next to her, and she was clapping with hands raised above her head. Everyone kept applauding until Mr. B raised a hand for silence.

"I think Adam should play his encore now!" The audience laughed. Mr. B turned to Adam. "How about something special for your grandmother?"

"Of course!" He would play Grandma's favorite song. Calming his breath, he checked his strings, fixed his eyes on Little Jabari, and began . . . "We and the Moon Are Neighbors." After the first verse, the audience began singing and humming along.

People crowded around Adam with congratulations. He caught Mama's eye as she smiled at him from the center of another whirl of people. But while he was saying "thank you, thank you," his heart was pounding. Where was the famous violinist? What did she think? Was his plan just too far-fetched? Had his imagination gone crazy after reading about a horse of power? It was one thing to make beautiful music, but why would the Permitteds care about that? The more these questions reeled in his head, the more his smiles felt hollow.

Gradually, the crowd thinned until he could see Grandma still in her seat in the front row. Ms. Roth was sitting next to her, and they seemed deep in conversation.

Leila and the girl from the photo stood nearby, chatting in the shadowy glow cast by the lights above the stage. He couldn't see his mother or Mr. B. Other music students had packed their instruments away and some were already leaving with their families. He needed to fetch his violin case. He returned to the stage to make his way into the building, but before he could reach it, Mr. B appeared in the light of the arched doorway. Mama was with him, and so was a woman whose hair was tied in a long wavy ponytail. He couldn't stop a gasp. Her long hair shone in the same chestnut color as he imagined the coat of the real Jabari!

Even before Mr. B had introduced him, the famous violinist was extending her hand.

"Thank you so much, Adam!" Her voice was lilting and warm. "You transported me to a springtime valley that I didn't want to leave! May I look at your violin?"

Later, Adam would remember how gently she held his violin, praising its sound as well as admiring Little Jabari. She asked him to take her to meet Grandma. However, most of the conversation became lost in the haze of the evening. It was Mama, Leila, and Grandma who later filled in the details for him as they sat around the table with cups of hot chocolate and mint tea before going to bed. The famous violinist had promised to do what she could. Mama said the publicity might help. Or it might make the people who decided on permits "dig in their heels." Adam's face must have fallen.

"But whatever happens, Adam," said Mama, "you were very brave. Your father would have said you were shining a light—"

"On Zak as well," Leila interjected.

"And with your violin . . ." Grandma paused, breathing softly. ". . . you let us all dream."

LEILA

QUESTIONS

Dear Uncle Elias,

I can't sleep and I have SO much to tell you! A famous violinist from OverSeas came to our music school concert tonight and she loved Adam's playing! She spoke to us afterward. (By the way, she puts her hair in a high ponytail like I sometimes do!) She said that some Non students are going to study with other music students for a month in her city—and she wants Adam to be one of them!

We are so proud of Adam, although today was also a terrible day. Do you know that Zak was sent to prison for THREE years? It was so horrible in the court when they took him away. Zak tried to be brave but I'm sure he was really scared.

I don't know how Adam played SO well when he was really upset but you should have heard how the audience clapped and clapped! Then Adam came to the front of the stage and told EVERYONE that Mama could be sent over the Wall. He also talked about Zak. None of us knew that he was going to do that.

The famous musician says she has a friend who's a journalist and she's going to ask him to write about Adam and what will happen if the Permitteds don't give Mama her permit. Mama thanked her, although I don't think she believes that those Permitteds will care. But Grandma says we mustn't give up hope and that there's always tomorrow. I hope she's right.

I am sure that Mama has already told you about the lawyer, Ms. Roth, who got Adam back from the police. She's a Permitted, but she hates the injustice and can be very fierce. Uncle Musa says she did her best even though she couldn't stop Zak from being sent to prison. To tell you the truth, I was scared of Ms. Roth at first, but now I know that she's really nice. She brought her granddaughter to Adam's concert. Her name is Rachel and she said she loved it! She learns the cello, but she's never performed in a concert. You know how Mama says I'm a chatterbox? Well, you should hear Rachel! She said if she could come to our music school, then we could play our instruments together. Maybe she gets crazy ideas like me.

Uncle Elias, I think of you every time I draw or write in the book you gave me. Sometimes I just write a question when I don't know the answer. Here are a few:

- How can people be so cruel?
- Why do some Permitted children look frightened of me when I'm just playing my flute to a parakeet? Why can't they be like Rachel?
- Will Zak believe that there's always tomorrow?

If you have any answers, please tell me.
Your loving niece,
Leila

ADAM

DREAMS

MEMORIES OF THE DAY FLOODED back as Adam pulled on his pajamas. Good moments from his concert jostled with awful ones of Zak in court . . . but it was when he began imagining Zak curled up on a prison bed that he knew he had to quiet his mind before he could sleep. Grandfather's violin lay nestled in its open case on the top shelf above his books. It was too late to play. Instead, he found Uncle Elias's book tucked beneath the folktales from Dad. . . .

MY DREAM

In my grandparents' valley,
A chestnut horse leads us to the stream.
The sun shines and birds sing.
We drink from the spring.

In my grandparents' valley,
There are no men with guns.
The sun shines and birds sing.
We play together, oud and violin.

One day in every valley,
there will be no guns, no walls, no permits.
The sun will shine and birds will sing.
One day.

AUTHOR'S NOTE

Journey to Jo'burg, my first novel, opened a window to a world that was otherwise unknown to most young readers in the UK and US in the mid-1980s. It was banned in apartheid South Africa until Nelson Mandela's release from jail, but the story of two Black children seeking their mother found readers across the globe and has stayed in print. While readers' responses have ranged over the years from wanting me to verify its reality to commenting on universal elements of the story, they have always reflected a hunger to empathize, understand, and ask deeper questions.

Thirty-five years later, I have felt compelled to write another novel that opens a window that has been mostly shut . . . and to let readers hear voices they rarely, if ever, hear. For many years, I, too, didn't hear them until, thanks to the British Council, I was given the opportunity to meet young Palestinian readers. The philosophical nature of their questions struck deep chords, e.g., "Black children and white children both like the color of flowers. What is your opinion on this?" and "Is Justice sleeping or is it a dream? If Justice is sleeping, who will wake Justice up?"

Children of the Stone City is my fictional response to these two profound questions. In between four author visits to the Occupied Territories and Jordan (spanning 2000 to 2016), I have read widely, especially Palestinian and Israeli writers on human rights. I also turned to organizations such as Amnesty International, B'Tselem, and Defence for Children International to learn more, especially about the lives of children.

Since childhood, I have loved the directness and universality of ancient myths and tales that reflect our worst and our best selves. The ancient Stone City of my story's setting is unnamed and its people are simply identified as Permitteds and Nons. The two categories can be found in societies around the world. I hope readers may be stirred to think about the consequences for all children in societies powerfully divided into Permitteds and Nons. The UN Convention on the Rights of the Child requires equality! I have also minimized references to religion in order to strip my story to its core: the behavior of one human being to another.

At its heart, *Children of the Stone City* is about music-loving Non siblings, Adam and Leila, who are desperate for their mother not to be taken away—sent away—across the Wall. Moreover, in this society, what will happen with a high-spirited Non boy like their friend Zak? While the viewpoints shift between Adam and Leila, both Uncle Yosef and Ms. Roth are Permitteds who refuse to have their humanity limited in a society based on permits. My concerns about this division between Permitteds and Nons stem from being born in South Africa, where I was classified at birth as a "Permitted." My birth certificate states "Race: European." Had I been born in Occupied Europe in 1943, with my Jewish mother, I would have been classified as a "Non."

Finally, weaving music into *Children of the Stone City* has been part of my dreaming about this story from its beginning. Music doesn't know Permitteds and Nons because it speaks to our hearts. Music leaps over and seeps through walls. Music cannot be confined. From the darkest dungeon, it can sing about the light beyond and the sky above us all. It offers hope.

ACKNOWLEDGMENTS

The journey that led me to write *Children of the Stone City* has been a long one. I am thankful for the creative vision of the British Council Literature Programme that, from the 1990s, enabled me to work with writers for young people and meet readers in various parts of Africa and the Middle East.

I also thank the International Board on Books for Young People (IBBY), conceived by Jella Lepman after the devastation of World War II. Founded on the belief of the power of books to expand children's lives through imagining and connecting with the lives of others, IBBY now brings together over eighty national sections across the globe. IBBY has encouraged many conversations, crossing many boundaries. I owe special thanks to IBBY Palestine and its president, Jehan Helou, for enabling me to meet young Palestinians, including readers of the Arabic edition of *Journey to Jo'burg*. They were all passionate about discussing equality, justice, and racism. The philosophical nature of some of their questions sowed the seeds for this novel and its allegorical form.

The questions in my Author's Note were posed to me in UNRWA's Al Nuzha School for Girls in a refugee camp on the outskirts of Amman in September 2001. For that unforgettable visit, I thank Matar Saqer, public information officer at UNRWA, and the British Council in Jordan.

Since childhood, thanks to my parents, music has enriched and expanded my world. I am grateful to the Edward Said National Conservatory of Music, whose talented young musicians I first heard in London through its project with the City of London Choir. My thanks go as well to PalMusicUK. I also thank Sarum Concern for Israel/Palestine for its enlightening program of musical and discussion events in the precincts of Salisbury Cathedral, with special thanks to Sharen Green for the introduction.

I am indebted to many people who have offered me insights along my journey, and I apologize if I haven't named everyone. For their kindness and patience in responding to my many queries, I thank Samia Khoury, author of *Reflections from Palestine: A Journey of Hope*; Zakaria Odeh, director of the Civic Coalition for Palestinian Rights in Jerusalem; and the late Samar Qutob, translator of *Journey to Jo'burg*. For enlarging my understanding of the experiences of young people in particular, I thank Ayed Abu Eqtaish of Defence for Children International; Nadera Shalhoub-Kevorkian, Lawrence D. Biele Chair in Law, Hebrew University of Jerusalem; Nurit Peled-Elhanan, Professor of Language Education, Hebrew University of Jerusalem; as well as the team at the Tamer Institute for Community Education in Ramallah.

I thank Tamer for introducing me to schools where the children's capacity to retain hope for peace and justice was heartening: Collège des Frères and St. George's School in East Jerusalem; and Al-Haj Ma'zouz Al-Masri School for Girls in Nablus. I also thank Samia Khoury for introducing me to Rawdat El-Zuhur (Garden of Flowers) School, East Jerusalem. The light in those young eyes remains with me alongside the dark shadows in the eyes of former child detainees.

I am also indebted to a number of NGOs for their reports concerned with human rights, including B'Tselem, HaMoked, Society of St. Yves, and Amnesty International.

I thank Nora Kort for her personal tour of the Wujoud Museum, offering an intimate window into cultural history, and my thanks to Professor Sharif Kanaana for *Speak, Bird, Speak Again: Palestinian Arab Folktales*, coauthored with Professor Ibrahim Muhawi. My thanks, too, to Shadia Helou for her kindness in offering accommodation in Ramallah.

I have been most fortunate in readers who have sustained and challenged me during the course of my drafts. I thank Sophie Hallam, who believed in Adam, Leila, and Zak even when I was enticed to put them aside for a while so I could work with her as editor on my retelling of *Cinderella of the Nile*. For their valuable comments, I thank Debbie Epstein, Jamila Gavin, Jehan Helou, Madeleine Lake, Jane Nissen, Shereen Pandit, and Jessica Powers. I owe special thanks to artistic director Sharon Muiruri Coyne for her ongoing inquiries about the welfare of my children in the Stone City. Knowing that "my children" felt alive and mattered to her has been important.

I am deeply grateful to Rosemary Brosnan and Courtney Stevenson at HarperCollins USA and Michelle Misra at HarperCollins UK, as well as their publishing teams, for all their support. My thanks go also to Hilary Delamere and Jessica Hare at The Agency.

Finally, I was fortunate to have my husband, Nandha, at my side on my author visits in 2000–2001; he confirmed that he had seen what I had seen, and we shared experiences and discussed them long afterward. As ever, I thank him for his companionship and constant support in accompanying me on this journey.